Dear Reader,

Do *you* have a secret fantasy? Everyone does.
Maybe it's to be rich and famous and beautiful. Or
to start a no-strings affair with a sexy mysterious
stranger. Or to have a sizzling second chance with a
former sweetheart.... You'll find these dreams—and
much more—in Temptation's exciting new yearlong
promotion, Secret Fantasies!

Bestselling Harlequin author Kathleen O'Brien
kicks off the series in January 1995 with the emotional,
dramatic *Memory Lapse*. Hero Drew's fantasy is the
return of his gorgeous ex-fiancée, Laura. And Drew
would give *anything* to make his fantasy come true...

In the coming months look for Secret Fantasies
books by Debra Carroll, Glenda Sanders and
JoAnn Ross. Please write and let us know how you
enjoy the "fantasy."

Happy Reading!

The Editors

c/o Harlequin Temptation
225 Duncan Mill Road
Don Mills, Ontario
M3B 3K9

Dear Reader,

Once upon a time, long before I thought of writing novels, I fell in love with a fictional man I called a "hero." Pieced together from stories I heard and movies I watched, he was a handsome figure clad in shining armor, sword raised high to fight for love and honor.

Of course, even then I knew it took more than bulging muscles and tempered steel to create this paragon. Young as I was, I sensed that the true test of a hero lies in his attitude toward the woman he loves. A real hero will brave any danger for his lady's sake. He has spent his life cultivating courage, endurance and brawn merely so that he can, when the time comes, use them to rescue her.

Over the years, I have also learned that heroes come in all sizes and shapes, all ages and occupations—and in both genders. I have seen these remarkable people and have been filled with awe and gratitude for their daily courage. But somehow, through it all, my fantasy hero survived in my imagination, standing ready to face any peril for the woman he loves.

So when I was asked to write the story of a "secret fantasy," what could be more natural than having this hero step forward? Though Drew Townsend, the hero of *Memory Lapse,* is a contemporary man, he is as dedicated to rescuing his lady as Lancelot ever was. Drew's ex-fiancée, Laura Nolan, is a prisoner of her past, and when she comes to him for help, he cannot fail her.

I hope you enjoy reading the story of Drew's "secret fantasy" half as much as I enjoyed writing it. And I hope that when you compare him to the "hero" who surely lives on in your imagination, too, you'll recognize what made him so special to me.

Sincerely,

Kathleen O'Brien

"I walk in my sleep."

Drew frowned, bewildered by the tension in Laura's voice. "But lots of people sleepwalk—"

"Not the way I do. I get up, I go downstairs, sometimes I even go outside…and then I take off my clothes."

Fear shone in her eyes and there was a desperate quiver to her lips. She looked seventeen. The same age she'd been the first time they'd tried to make love.…

"I'm naked, Drew."

He cursed and moved away from her toward the window. The snow was falling heavily now, piling in the corners of the window. Naked in the snow. Oh, God.…

Kathleen O'Brien, who lives in Florida, started out as a newspaper feature writer, but after marriage and motherhood, she traded that in to write novels full-time. Kathleen likes strong heroes who overcome adversity, which is probably the result of her reading all those classic, tragic novels when she was younger. However, being a true romantic, she prefers *her* stories to end happily!

Don't miss any of our special offers. Write to us at the following address for information on our newest releases.

Harlequin Reader Service
U.S.: 3010 Walden Ave., P.O. Box 1325, Buffalo, NY 14269
Canadian: P.O. Box 609, Fort Erie, Ont. L2A 5X3

MEMORY LAPSE
KATHLEEN O'BRIEN

Harlequin Books

TORONTO • NEW YORK • LONDON
AMSTERDAM • PARIS • SYDNEY • HAMBURG
STOCKHOLM • ATHENS • TOKYO • MILAN
MADRID • WARSAW • BUDAPEST • AUCKLAND

To Ann Bair
For friendship that regularly goes above and beyond

ISBN 0-373-25622-1

MEMORY LAPSE

Copyright © 1995 by Kathleen O'Brien.

1

SOMEONE WAS CRYING.

The sound was feeble, just a few thin notes of help-less misery, like the muffled sobbing of a child who has given up hope of being comforted. Laura might not even have heard it, except that the midnight air caught the sobs in its glassy web, suspending them above her with an unnatural, frozen clarity.

Such desolate sounds. Cold bands of pity tightened around Laura's chest, squeezing until she could hardly breathe. Who would make a child cry like that? Why did no one go to her? Why did no one pick her up, warm her, reassure her? She was so unhappy, so un-bearably alone.

Laura knew she should do something. It had snowed today, and the girl was very cold. But it was so dark, so hard to move her strangely aching limbs, and ev-erything was so confusing. She wasn't sure where the little girl was, or who she was, or whether somehow *she* was the girl, or whether this was all some horrible nightmare from which she must wake up....

"No!" Though her eyes had already been open, star-ing uncomprehendingly at the formless white world around her, Laura was suddenly jolted into awareness by a piercing sense of panic. Her heart thudded high in her throat, and she realized that she had been asleep. The sad little girl must have been a dream. And yet it hadn't been a dream, not quite.

Her eyes darted frantically across the snow-shrouded shapes, trying to identify them, though her mind was still fuzzy, clouded with fear and confusion. Where was she? Were those white, reaching arms just tree branches? Was that hulking form only a lawn chair? She shivered, the cold, aching pain in her chest intensifying. Where was she? She couldn't be back in Albany, back at Winterwalk, could she? But how could she *not* be there? Obviously she'd been sleepwalking, and she had never done that anywhere but Winterwalk.

No! She shook her head, trying to clear it. No, no, no. It was crazy to think that, even in these terrifying fugue states, she could possibly be spirited back to Winterwalk. It was a thousand miles away. She hadn't been there in years. And she would never go there again.

She would never again stand under the shadow of the thrusting tower, snow-swept colonnades and leering gargoyles of Winterwalk, the eerie Venetian Gothic villa she had once called home. She had fled from there three years ago, leaving behind, like thwarted ghosts, the strange compulsions that haunted her sleep.

In her desperation, she had left other things at Winterwalk, too. She'd left innocence and hope and love. She'd left Drew Townsend's diamond ring, tucked into an incoherent, inadequate note she knew he'd never understand.

But, for that sacrifice, she had believed she was buying freedom. Safety. Here in Boston, in her boring, rubber-stamp town house, she was supposed to be safe from this madness in the middle of the night.

So why, after three years of peace, had the sleepwalking started again? Why tonight? She took a deep, shaking breath of icy air, though it scoured her nose and throat like sandpaper, and tried to orient herself. How long had she been out here? Her lungs hurt, as if from a prolonged struggle to breathe. Her feet were bare and growing numb. When she touched her fingers to her face, she felt a lacework of frost where unchecked tears had frozen on her cheeks.

What else had she done? Her trembling fingers dropped to her nightgown, feeling clumsily for the buttons that should have been closed tightly around her neck, dreading what she knew she would find.

And she was right. Her throat was bare, as cold and unyielding as marble. Her fingers fluttered downward, down across her collarbone, her breastbone, the shivering plane of her stomach. All the buttons were undone, and the edges of her gown fluttered open, exposing her to the frigid wind. Snow blew against the swell of her breast, and her body wasn't even warm enough to melt the tiny flakes that piled against her pale skin, as if trying to cover her nakedness.

Oh, God. She wrenched the gown closed with half numb fingers as hot tears ran alongside the frozen ones. It was true, then. It had started again. She knew all too well what would have happened if she hadn't managed to wake up. She would have removed the nightgown, cast it aside, white on white, silk on snow. She would have knelt on the ground, weeping, and then . . .

And then what? From the time she was ten years old, whenever she had walked in her sleep her mother had followed her, put a blanket around her shivering body and led her gently into the house. But her mother had died a month ago, and now Laura was alone.

Completely alone in her "safe" little Boston town house that suddenly wasn't safe at all, where the old ghosts could still pluck her out of her bed and toss her out into the cruel winter night, where she might easily have frozen to death.

Choking on her terrified tears, clutching her gown, she stumbled on numb feet up the stairs that led to her tiny kitchen. She rattled the doorknob frantically, her fingers awkward, the cold metal uncooperative. "Open. Please, open." The words blew out on a gust of milky vapor, hung in the frozen air like an echo, then disappeared. "Please." She moaned, struggling with the doorknob as if her life depended on it.

The latch finally gave way, and with a low sob she flung herself into the warm kitchen, where the range gleamed reassuringly under the hood light, and the blue liquid crystal display of the microwave clock glowed steadily in the corner.

Breathing heavily, she leaned against the door. Her whole body hurt now that she was warmer, as pulsing waves of hot blood tried to shove through frozen veins. She stared at the room as if she'd never seen it before, though just hours ago this kitchen had seemed a haven, this town house a refuge.

For three years she had lived a compulsively normal life here, tacking up bouquets of cinnamon so her kitchen would smell like the pies her mother had never baked, subscribing to *TV Guide* though she hated television, going to work every day though she'd inherited more money than any human could ever spend. She clipped coupons, filled her hall closet with spare light bulbs and Band-Aids, and planted geraniums on the front stoop, as if these things were talismans, charms with which she could exorcise her past.

Now she saw how naive those measures had been. Even such an ordinary existence couldn't camouflage her. Somehow the ghosts or the memories or the madness—or whatever it was that haunted her sleep at Winterwalk—had found her here just the same. Nothing could keep them away—not doors or distance, not charms or cookies, neither locks nor life-style. There was, finally, nowhere to hide.

And then, as the frozen tears began to melt and run down her cheeks as if being wept all over again, she knew what she had to do. Though she hated Winterwalk, though it represented every nightmare she feared and every dream she'd lost, she knew she had to go back.

TILTING HIS CHAIR and tapping his Montblanc against his temple absently, Drew Townsend stared, half hypnotized, at the snowflakes that drifted past his office window. When he had rented Winterwalk a year ago, he'd deliberately chosen the second-story tower rooms for his office and bedroom, so that his windows had the best view of any of the twenty-five rooms, overlooking terraced gardens and sparkling fountains that spread out around the huge circular front drive.

At the time, he hadn't realized how distracting the view could be. From the other side of his desk, his secretary's intensely feminine voice, as feather light and languorous as the snowflakes, was detailing his commitments for the day, but he could hardly force himself to listen.

He sighed as Ginger drawled on. How many years, he wondered vaguely, did it take a woman to perfect the art of saying "variable rate liability" as if it were the most exotic sex toy on the market?

The tapping of his pen quickened, beating an impatient tattoo. It's only business meetings and financial news, he found himself thinking irritably. Just get on with it. But immediately he was ashamed. It wasn't Ginger's fault he was perversely annoyed by her manner today. Ginger was just being Ginger, which, nine days out of ten, was exactly what Drew wanted her to be.

She wasn't the first resolutely flirtatious, unabashedly sexual girlfriend he'd had in the past three years. She was, if anyone was counting, the fourth. He seemed to seek out elegantly trashy women who loved sex and didn't mind showing it. That made sense, he supposed, after the fiasco with Laura. At least with a Ginger you knew where you stood. You knew that as long as you kept the sex exciting, the wine vintage and the trinkets eighteen karat, Ginger would be there. She wouldn't bolt in the middle of the night, leaving a note full of lies propped against the mantel like some modern-day Jane Eyre.

No, he damned well didn't want to get involved in anything like that again. But, even so, sometimes he found the Gingers of his life strangely unsatisfying. They seemed as insubstantial as the snowflakes. They lulled him, numbed him, but when he reached out to capture their essence, his hand closed around nothingness.

"Are you even listening to me, mister?"

Ginger's voice came from just over his shoulder, and he wondered guiltily how long ago he'd tuned her out. Quite a while, he surmised from the throaty, teasing exasperation in her voice. *Get mad, Ginger*, he thought suddenly, surprising himself, since obviously he didn't really want a scene. *I've been rude as hell.*

Don't let me get away with it.

But of course she didn't get angry—she never did. Bending over the back of his chair, she put her well-cared-for hands on his shoulders and began to massage with slow, kneading strokes. "What is it?" she purred. "Feeling tense?"

She was leaning so low he could see her silky blond hair draped across his shirt, and her breath softly blew the scent of gardenias against his temple. Within seconds her movements took on a blatantly seductive quality, her hands feathering down the front of his shirt to pull free one button, slide in and rub across his chest.

He managed the obligatory contented murmur, but in truth he hardly felt anything she did. His mind was still drifting, like the snowflakes that glided aimlessly past the window and landed on the sculpted hedges. Everything out there was white and utterly still, as if it had been placed under a magic spell that mesmerized him, as well.

When a red-checkered cab suddenly appeared at the edge of Winterwalk's long drive, it was as conspicuous in this pristine landscape as a bloodstain. But even that didn't pique his interest much. Letting Ginger's hands roam unnoticed, he merely watched the cab's progress as it rolled slowly toward Winterwalk, leaving two long ribbons in its wake. He couldn't even rouse himself enough to wonder who it was.

As if confused by his continued passivity, Ginger grew bolder. She stroked the length of his arms suggestively, and taking his right hand in hers, she brought it up and cupped it over her breast.

Automatically Drew's hand tightened, and Ginger leaned into his palm, filling it with warm, silk-covered flesh. "Umm," she murmured as he rolled his fingers slowly. "Oh, Drew."

But even as he dutifully performed the expected maneuvers, Drew was suddenly aware of nothing but the cab, which had finally come to a stop in front of Winterwalk. Its passenger was getting out, and Drew stared, his heart racing strangely, some sixth sense prickling. The languid spell was broken, and he felt, for the first time today, fully awake, almost hyperaware as he watched the passenger emerge tentatively and search in her purse for the fare.

She wore a heavy blue woolen coat, which rendered her figure nearly anonymous. Above that, a blue scarf and a black hat cloaked her face, as if she didn't want to be recognized. But something twisted in Drew's gut as, dropping her small suitcase on the ground next to her, the young woman turned toward the house. Slowly she lifted her pale face, scanning the house from terrace to tower, from the conservatory at the south end to the ballroom at the north, as if ticking every detail off against some internal checklist.

Could it be? As Drew gazed down on that pale, unsmiling oval, which was still too far away for features to be clearly distinguished, his hand dropped from Ginger's breast. Ignoring her mew of disappointment, he rose stiffly from his chair, his pen tumbling unnoticed to the carpet.

Oh, God. He could have sworn the woman was looking up at the very window where he stood, though he knew the sun, which at high noon glinted blindingly off the casements, hid him from her view. Even so, he could have sworn her soft gray-blue eyes—he knew they were the softest, saddest eyes in New York State, though he couldn't see them from here at all—were staring straight into his. Suddenly his chest tightened, and his knees began to tingle, as if he needed to move, to run . . .

But somehow, with an enormous effort, he forced himself to stand still while his brain tried to process the information this electrifying bolt of adrenaline was sending him.

Laura Nolan had come home.

LAURA MUST HAVE stood on the veined marble terrace for a full five minutes, just looking up at Winterwalk, trying to gather the courage to approach the front door. She stood so long the cold began to seep through the seams of her boots and gloves, but still she couldn't move, hypnotized by the house, which was somehow both achingly familiar and startlingly new.

She had always, even as a child, been ambivalent about her amazing home. Officially Winterwalk's architecture was "eclectic," a labyrinthine blend of Venetian and Turkish elements that defied categorization. To Laura, though, it had seemed half storybook castle and half pure, screaming nightmare.

Intricate cornices dripped from a complicated stagger of terra-cotta roofs; balconies with elaborate balustrades hung from arched windows and doors; gargoyles lunged from every peak and corner, frozen forever in their postures of agony or aggression.

Now, after her three-year absence, Winterwalk seemed more nightmarish than ever. Had the roofline always been so heavily crested, baring jagged teeth against the innocent blue sky? And she hadn't remembered that the tall, thin tower was quite so strange, the outdoor staircase winding around it like a snake prepared to squeeze its prey.

She shivered, averting her eyes. She hated Winterwalk. Hated it. She wished suddenly, intensely, that it would disappear, that it would miraculously be struck by lightning and burn to the ground. It was a horrible house. Why on earth had anyone built it? And why, why, why, after all that had happened between them, did Drew Townsend want to live here?

He had always adored Winterwalk, she remembered, though she had never been able to fathom why. He had been born at Springfields, the neoclassical estate next door, which to the envious Laura had seemed the embodiment of grace and purity. When she had questioned him, he had explained that he found Winterwalk "whimsical" and "stimulating," words that seemed utterly foreign to her.

But nothing frightened Drew, not even Winterwalk. He had made fun of the fiercest gargoyles—the ones that terrified Laura most—giving them absurd names like Fifi and Thumper and Bucko. "No peeking, boys," he would warn the contorted, malevolent faces, and then, laughing, he would turn to kiss the pinched worry from Laura's lips.

Her heart tightened, and with a sense of defeat she bent over to pick up her suitcase. She couldn't go in. How could she enter a house that was so full of painful memories? She could almost feel Drew's kisses now, nipping, playful, then harder, more insistent . . .

Suddenly the heavy walnut door in front of her swung wide on its hinges. Laura froze in the act of turning away, her suitcase half hoisted, her awkward pose as guilty and ridiculous as if she had been caught stealing the silver tea service.

For a moment she could see nothing in the yawning shadow of the open doorway. And then Drew Townsend walked out onto the terrace.

"Hello, Laura." His deep voice was neither warm nor cold, containing neither welcome nor rebuff, and she couldn't detect, in that careful neutrality, even a hint of surprise. How was that possible? He should be shocked. Three years ago, she had left him a note that had sworn she'd never, never come back.

She didn't know what to say. She had been prepared, she thought, for any amount of anger, but somehow this calm indifference took her breath away.

When she didn't answer, he moved farther out onto the patio, and recognition dragged at her heart. He looked exactly the same. Perhaps even more handsome. The bright winter sun drove spears of fire deep into his thick chestnut hair and lit the soft moss green of his eyes to an emerald sparkle.

But what had she expected? He was only twenty-seven. Three years could hardly have robbed him of his looks. Had she imagined that his broken heart would dig furrows of pain into his long face, hollowing out the line under his strong cheekbones?

Or had she merely hoped that those three years would render her immune to his too-potent sexual charm? If so, she'd been hopelessly naive. Just ten seconds in his presence, and already she could feel the low throb, the primitive drumbeat of desire that had tormented her for years.

"Let me take that." He slid the suitcase from her fingers, and her hand fell uselessly to her side, but she didn't move. For a long moment they stared at each other while snowflakes swirled around them, catching on the cotton of his sleeves, on the fiery brown of his hair.

She couldn't imagine what her expression must be, but his was appraising, thoughtful. His eyes were narrowed, squinting against the sun speculatively, as if she was an unwieldy package that had been left at his doorstep by mistake. As if, now that she was here, he couldn't quite figure out what to do with her.

When he finally spoke, it was with a hint of impatience.

"Well?" He gestured toward the still open door. "Are you coming in?"

She nodded slowly, not knowing what else to do, but she didn't follow him as he walked briskly toward the house. She felt as coldly immobile as the marble statues that had once stood amid the greenery in Winterwalk's conservatory.

Just as he reached the door, she called out to stop him. "Drew!"

He swiveled, surprised and clearly annoyed to see that she had not yet moved.

"Drew," she said again, trying not to sound frantic. She had to clear this up before they went inside. He hadn't asked why she was here, not even when he saw the suitcase. "Drew, I'm not really back."

He tilted his head, raising his dark brows. "You're not?"

She flushed and awkwardly swept snowflakes from her lashes. "I mean, I'm not back for good."

He didn't speak. His body was rigid, unmoving.

"Do you understand what I mean?" She wound her gloved fingers together and pressed them against her stomach, where the familiar aching throb was still pounding its message through her veins. "I'm not coming back to—" To *you*, she almost said. To *us*. "To stay."

"Of course not," he said, his voice still reflecting nothing but impatience. "But I'd rather hear exactly why you *are* here in the comfort of a heated room. You're nicely bundled up for a long chat in the snow, but you may have noticed that I'm not."

Yes, she'd noticed. His dark brown corduroy pants and fawn-colored shirt looked quite comfortable for working indoors, but he probably was freezing out here. The wind molded the fabric against his chest, outlining his muscular torso. Strangely, the middle button of his shirt had come undone, and she wondered if the snow was drifting through the opening.

Suddenly, before she could speak, there was a flurry of activity in the doorway, and a shockingly beautiful blonde in a stylish pink coat appeared at Drew's side.

"Well, your lawyer didn't like it one bit, Drew," the woman said, apparently unaware that she had interrupted anything. Her tone was intimate, scolding and seductive all at once. "But he finally agreed to reschedule. Honestly, Drew, I think you've made everyone in Albany mad, canceling appointments like this, but I did it. Your day is clear."

She ran long, pink-tipped fingers through Drew's hair, brushing off a haze of snowflakes. "So, if you really don't need me, I'm off for a facial." Scooping up his hand, she ran the tips of his fingers along her cheek. "All this snow has simply parched my skin."

Drew frowned, but the woman's flow of honeyed verbiage didn't slow. Looking up with a surprised expression, she appeared to notice Laura for the first time. "Hello," she said silkily, letting Drew's hand drop from her face but hanging on to it nonetheless. "I'm Ginger Belmont, Drew's secretary. You must be Laura Nolan. I've seen your pictures upstairs, and of course there's the famous marble head in the conservatory. Though you look older now, naturally. You were just a kid when you posed for that, weren't you?"

"Ginger." Drew broke in quietly but firmly, easing his hand away with a deliberate restraint. He didn't

look as if he found Ginger's frothy chatter at all amus-
ing. Laura would have hated to see that irritable look
turned her way.

But the blonde wasn't a bit chastened or perhaps she
didn't notice. She was eyeing Laura carefully. "You must
be here to talk about the lease? Or dare I hope you've
decided to sell?" Her voice dipped conspiratorially.
"You just don't know how eager Drew is to buy this
place. He loves it here, don't you, Drew?"

Ginger turned to him for confirmation, and suddenly noticing the open button, she gave a small, gasping laugh. "Oops," she said with a charming moue of
embarrassment, reaching out to slide the button
through its hole expertly. "That's better." She patted
Drew's chest. "Well, I'll leave you two to go over things.
Nice to meet you, Laura."

And then, like a brightly colored bird that had landed
only briefly before flitting away again, she was gone.
But, on second thought, the bird image didn't really fit,
did it? Something bigger, perhaps. More dangerous.
Laura felt slightly dazed, as if she had just been man-
handled by an expert—sized up, roughed up and
warned off.

The signs had been unmistakable. Ginger Belmont
was more than a secretary to Drew. Much more. Her
hands, her eyes, even her voice, had slithered all over
him.

And that button. Only a complete fool could miss the
implications of that button.

Suddenly Laura's heart felt so tight she couldn't
breathe. She could hear, as if the echo had been trapped
here at Winterwalk three years ago, the desolate,
hopeless sound of her own tears, and Drew's husky,
troubled voice trying to calm her. "It's all right," he had

said brokenly, his fingers closing the buttons on her blouse as rapidly as they could. "It's all right, Laura, I swear it is." He had pulled her shaking body to him fiercely, stroking her hair. "I love you, sweetheart, don't you know that? Just let me hold you. The rest of it doesn't matter." As she sobbed into his chest, his voice over her head had grown harsh, as if he was forcing himself to believe his own words. "I can wait. Or, if I have to, I can live without it, Laura. I swear to God I can. I just can't live without *you*."

Laura had recognized the desperate chivalry with which he'd made that vow but she had known, even then, that it wasn't true. How could a man live without sex? Especially a man like Drew, whose potent virility was, particularly at that moment, inarguable. She couldn't even think of asking him to marry a woman whose fear of sex was so irrational and yet hopelessly insurmountable.

But still, seeing Ginger touch him so intimately, knowing that she was giving Drew all the pleasure Laura had never been able to offer him, filled Laura with an unaccountable fury. She watched the pink coat disappear around the back of the house, heard a motor start and rev away and felt a painful though unwarranted sense of betrayal.

"So," she said, her voice thin and strangely unpleasant, "I see you decided celibacy wasn't for you, after all."

Drew's face hardened, the line of his mouth tightening.

"Just following orders, ma'am," he said, his tones clipped. His hands were folded into white-knuckled fists. "Isn't that what you told me to do? To forget about you? To find a woman without hang-ups, a woman who could 'really' love me?"

"And does she?" Laura whispered, knowing her face was as pale as the snow at her feet. Why was she asking? Why couldn't she stop caring? It wasn't any of her business, not anymore. "Does she?"

His unblinking gaze was stony, merciless. "Does she what? Have hang-ups?"

"No." Laura tried to will her voice to be stronger. "Does she love you?"

"You bet she does," he answered roughly. He narrowed his eyes against a gust of wind, and it gave him a sudden look of cold cruelty. "Like a pro."

2

LAURA'S REACTION took him by surprise. She didn't say a word, but her lips clamped together tightly, and her eyes widened, her forehead puckering slightly at the inner edge of her brows. At the sight, something nearly forgotten, something tender and protective, stirred in his gut.

God, he knew that expression, her wounded doe look, the essence of mute pain. And suddenly he felt almost ashamed. Perhaps he'd been too rough. But when she had so cavalierly dismissed any hope he might have been harboring about her motives for returning to Winterwalk, some bitterness he'd thought long dead had surfaced. He'd wanted to lash out, to hurt her in return.

To be fair to himself, though, he had spoken no more than the truth. Ginger was, in a way, Laura's own creation, and if Dr. Frankenstein didn't enjoy viewing her monster, that damn sure wasn't his fault.

He had done all a man could do to keep Laura from leaving. He had never forced her, never once implied that what she could give him wasn't enough. Over the three years of their engagement, he had stood under a thousand cold showers for her, had held at bay, night after night, a desire so tormenting it would have turned a less determined man into a ravaging beast. And he had been willing to go on suffering for as long as it took. Forever, if necessary.

He had been, in short, a fool. Damn it, that was all he needed to be ashamed of. The faint flicker of tenderness iced over as he remembered the wild misery of that last morning, when he'd found her note, explaining that she and her mother had left Winterwalk for good. Setting him "free," she'd called it, as if she was doing him a favor. God, what a stock cliché that was, and what a damned lie!

His fingers closed around the suitcase so tightly the leather creaked in protest. Free? All right, then, he was free to lose himself in the arms of a hundred Gingers if he wanted, at liberty to take without guilt whatever momentary release could be found in mindless sex. God damn it, he'd earned it.

The sun glinted off a dewy wetness along her lower lashes, and with effort he reined in his resentment. It was ridiculous getting steamed up like this after all these years. It was over, thank God—the years of gnawing frustration, and the three long years of betrayed anger that followed, too. Over. He mustn't let the sight of her agitate him, stirring up the muck of complicated emotions that had finally settled to the bottom.

Taking a deep breath of frigid air, he lifted the suitcase again. "Let's go in," he said curtly, "before we freeze."

This time she followed without protest, but he could sense her stiff discomfort as they entered the cavernous front hall. She walked gingerly, her soft boots making almost no sound as she crossed the checkerboard marble floor, as if she didn't want anyone to know she was there.

Drew watched her, puzzled. Whose attention could she be afraid of attracting? She must know that Drew lived here alone, with only a few day servants, gardeners and workmen and such. Even Ginger was gone, at least for today.

Perhaps she merely felt strange, being here now that it was no longer her home. But he hadn't changed anything—all the tapestries, Louis XVI chairs and Ming vases were in the same places they had always been. Winterwalk was as much museum as house, really, and he wouldn't have dreamed of fiddling with it. Only his bedroom and his office had been touched.

And besides, Laura's discomfort seemed deeper than interior decorating. It was as if her dislike of the house had intensified into— Into what? Hatred, he might have said, if it hadn't sounded so melodramatic.

She stood in the center of the front hall for a long time, her eyes wide and somber as she swept her gaze over the long second-floor balcony that looked down on them. She tucked her collar high up under her chin and kept staring, barely breathing, as though she expected to see something, someone, emerge from one of the rooms along those corridors.

Her anxiety was palpable. Drew's arms ached, tense with the stupid, instinctive urge to do what he would have done in the old days—take her into his arms, hold her, kiss her, warm her until he could feel her muscles relax. But that was impossible now. He just watched stonily, reminding himself that her moods weren't his problem anymore.

Finally she brought her gaze back to him, seeming suddenly to remember he was there, and as if that had been his cue, he reached for her coat. She resisted momentarily, clutching the lapels with white knuckles.

"Laura," he said softly. "You don't need this anymore."

His voice seemed to recall her to herself. With a sheepish smile, she loosened her grip. "Sorry," she murmured, relinquishing coat, hat and scarf with stilted courtesy.

Somehow, then, he got her into the living room, where he settled her on the most comfortable armchair and poured her three fingers of brandy. "To take the chill off," he said, nudging the glass against her limp hand.

Though he'd never known her to drink before, the offer obviously was welcome. Three or four sips later, her cheeks and lips had regained some color, and she actually relaxed enough to let her spine touch the back of the chair. Taking one more large swallow, then clearing her throat, she finally spoke.

"I need your help," she said, her voice strained but apparently under fairly firm control. "I know I haven't any right to ask, but I hope perhaps we can make a deal. You see, I don't have anyone else to ask. Mother died a month ago—"

She stopped, her control wavering, and took another sip of brandy. Drew took advantage of the pause to speak.

"Yes, I heard," he said. "I'm sorry." At the time, Drew had privately suspected Laura would be much happier without the querulous, suspicious, demanding woman hovering over her, but he had long ago learned not to voice such blasphemy. Though Laura had been adopted as an infant, she had never spoken of Elizabeth Nolan—had probably never even *thought* of her—as anything but a real mother, and she had been an unfailingly loyal daughter.

"Then you know I really am alone now," Laura went on, the stoicism in her face making the statement a fact, not a bid for pity. And it was true. Laura's natural parents had died in a car crash just after she was born, and her adoptive father, sculptor Damian Nolan, had abandoned the family when she was only ten.

"It's just that being alone makes it difficult for me to cope with—" she suddenly looked confused.

"With what?" he prompted her curiously. What practical skills did he possess for her to call on? He'd been blessed with a healthy inheritance, and since he'd known from childhood that his life would be spent managing the family's complicated investments, his education had all been in business and finance. Could she need money? Help with her portfolio? No, Laura's inheritance was as substantial as his, and somehow he couldn't imagine her coming back to Winterwalk after all these years just for tips on blue chips.

"It's awkward," she said. "I don't know how much you might have heard before. Mother tried to keep it quiet, but no one could keep a thing like this completely secret." She looked at her brandy glass, swirling it nervously. "Had you ever heard that I used to— that I had a sleep disorder?"

Now it was Drew's turn to be uncomfortable. Buying time, he slowly poured himself a brandy, wondering what his best answer would be. Of course he'd heard. Winterwalk servants constantly socialized with Springfields servants, and probably with workers on every other estate within gossiping distance. But once, when he had asked his sister about it, Stephanie had advised him never to mention it to Laura. Stephanie, though five years older than Laura, had been a close friend of hers, and she explained to Drew that Laura was embarrassed by her sleepwalking problem.

Anyway, Stephanie had assured him, it was really nothing. The doctor had checked it out and said that Laura would probably outgrow it. Because the rumors had soon stopped, Drew had vaguely assumed that was what had happened.

"I did hear something," he equivocated. "Sometimes, apparently, you walked in your sleep. It's a problem people often outgrow, isn't it?"

"Well, I didn't," she said, putting her glass on the end table and standing abruptly. With a blindly urgent motion she strode to the window, tunneling her hand into the brocaded draperies. "It happened again last night."

He frowned, bewildered by the tension in her voice. "Well, that's not so terrible, is it? Lots of people sleepwalk—"

"Not the way I do," she broke in, her voice thick and distorted. "You don't understand. I don't just walk in my sleep. I get up, I go downstairs, sometimes I even go outside. And then I take off my clothes."

Drew set his glass down slowly. "You do *what?*"

Without letting go of the drapes, she turned to face him. "I take my clothes off." Two high spots of color stained her cheeks, and her eyes were bright and feverish. "I'd never done it anywhere but at Winterwalk, never in my whole life. I was safe when I spent the night at a friend's house, when I went on vacation, when I was away at college. It never happened anywhere but here, never. I thought that as long as I didn't come home I would be safe."

Suddenly releasing the drapes, she clasped her arms around her chest, clutching her upper arms so tightly her fingers were buried in the soft wool of her sleeves.

"But I was wrong. Last night, in Boston, in the middle of the night, I went out into the snow and began to take off my nightgown."

With a growl of protest deep in his throat, Drew crossed the room to her.

"Laura . . ." But when he put his hands on her shoulders, she jerked away. He let his hands fall woodenly to his sides.

"No," she whispered, refusing to look at him. "Just listen." She bit her lower lip hard enough to leave two small ridges in the pink flesh. "I was all right. Just cold. And scared. Luckily I woke up before any real harm was done." She was talking rapidly, compulsively. "But now I know it can happen anywhere. It *will* happen anywhere and everywhere! And there's no one left to help me, to make sure I don't hurt myself—to make sure that no one *else* finds me like that, sees me like that"

Her voice was rising, growing shrill, and the sound pulled at something deep inside him. Instinct, habit— whatever it was, it seemed natural to hold her, to comfort her, but she had made it clear he had no right.

"What can I do?" He had meant to sound supportive, to banish her terror, but to his shock his voice was harsh. It was as if, when she drew away from him, she had loosened a tempest, a storm of remembered frustration, that now raged through him painfully.

He groaned under his breath. Not again. He hated this helpless feeling, the blood-maddening impotence, the shooting fear and adrenaline. Most of all he hated knowing he should save her, but knowing, too, that she would not let him.

"Damn it, what can I *do?*" he asked again. "I begged you before to go to a psychiatrist, but you wouldn't do it. Would it help to tell you that again? Would you go this time?"

"I went before," she began, her voice low.

"Twice!" He grabbed the edge of the draperies, just as she had done a moment ago, except that where she had seemed to be bracing herself, grounding herself, he was looking for somewhere to vent his unbearable frustration. He wanted to tear the blasted drapes right from the ceiling, to bury them both in an avalanche of red brocade. "Twice! Good God, Laura, you were completely sexually dysfunctional. Frigid! Did you really think two visits would cure you?"

She stared at him through eyes swimming in tears, her chin lifted high to try to keep them from spilling. But it was in vain—two huge, rainbowed drops overflowed and ran down her cheeks. Those tears were his only answer.

Of course, he didn't really need an answer. She had given him one three years ago. It had frightened her, she'd said. The psychiatrist had asked her questions, had tried to make her think about things, talk about things, and his insistence had terrified her as surely as Drew's touch on her bare skin ever did. She couldn't go back, she had said, weeping helplessly. She couldn't go back.

But though he'd mutely accepted her excuses then, swallowing his bitter disappointment, he found that he couldn't do so now.

"This is insane, Laura. I don't know what I can do for you. I've never known how to help you—don't you remember that? I've gone over it all a hundred times. A million." He dug his hands into his hair. "I told myself I should have done something else. Something... different. I don't know."

He didn't look at her, not wanting to see the tears that he knew were continuing to fall. "I tortured myself with should haves. I should have had you hypnotized. Or committed. I should never have touched you at all. I should have forced you. I should have threatened to leave—I should have made you marry me."

A humiliating sting pricked behind his eyes, and he dashed at a stack of books on the desk, sending one of them skidding across the polished mahogany with the back of his hand.

"I should have, I should have, I should have, until I nearly went crazy." His voice was raw. "And now, when I've finally stopped tormenting myself, you come back, asking if I'll help you with *another* problem? Can't you see how ridiculous that is?"

Finally he looked at her, half-ashamed of his outburst, expecting to see fear on her face. Instead, though her cheeks were runneled with shining tears, her gaze was steady. It was, paradoxically, as if his loss of control had allowed her to find her equilibrium.

"All I can see," she said, "is that I need help. Don't say no until you've heard me out, Drew. I said I had something to offer in return, and that's true. My mother's lawyers tell me you want to buy Winterwalk, but that she would never sell it to you. Well, I will."

He narrowed his eyes, forcing his heartbeat back under control. Could he have heard correctly? Was she trying to bribe him into accepting this bizarre assignment? Could she really believe a financial incentive would work where appeals to pity had not?

But he couldn't quite read her expression. He saw only intensity. Her eyes were as dark as cobalt, and her gaze seemed to bore into him like bits of glass.

"That's my deal. If you'll help me figure out why being in this house scares me so much, why it's here that I always walk in my sleep, then I'll sell it to you at any price you name."

"I don't need to own Winterwalk that badly," he said curtly. How little she understood what he had endured, if she really thought one crazy old mansion, however intriguing, would induce him to go through all that again! And he had no doubt that he *would* go through it again. If she was here, under his care, needy and helpless, it would be sheer torment. "I already live here. I have a ten-year lease, remember?"

They stared at each other a long moment, two poker players, each gauging the extent of the other's bluff. But her gaze fell first. And suddenly, as if she knew that she had played her only ace, her poise shattered.

"Oh, Drew," she cried, raw need on her face and in her voice. "Drew, please!"

Seen like this, with her defenses completely breached, she looked seventeen again, the same age she'd been the first time he'd tried to touch her. He could hardly bring himself to look at her. She had that same exposed fear shining in her eyes, that same desperate quiver at the edge of her lips.

He'd told himself back then that her reaction was perfectly normal, that the tears and breathless trembling were simply signs of sheltered innocence. It was much later that they realized it was something far, far worse.

"Drew, can't you see? Mother never told me much. I don't even really know what I do, not completely. It *has* to be someone I can trust. When I'm sleepwalking, I'm as vulnerable as a woman can be. I'm alone. I'm unconscious." She bit back a sob. "I'm naked, Drew."

Jesus. He cursed under his breath and moved away from her toward the window. The snow was falling heavily now, piling in the corners of the window. Naked in the snow. Oh, God . . .

"Can't you imagine how terrifying that is? I need someone I know would never hurt me. And you're the only one I have." She wiped the tears away with the heels of her hands. "I'm not asking for miracles, Drew. I'm only asking for a friend to watch out for me, to make sure I don't hurt myself, to see where I go, what I do and maybe, just maybe, help me figure out *why* I do it."

A friend. He nearly laughed at that, but it came out like a snort, an angry, bestial sound, so he cut it off abruptly, rubbing his hands across his face. A friend.

"All right," he said, his voice leaden, a condemned man's voice. "All right, Laura. We can give it a try."

AFTER THAT, without putting anything into words, they both seemed to call an emotional truce. Drew gave her a few minutes to pull herself together and then took her in to lunch.

Though Laura knew it was only the eye of the hurricane, she was extremely grateful for the respite. The pine refectory table was set with fresh flowers. The creamy tomato soup was piping hot, perfect for a snowy day, and the chicken breasts were grilled to perfection.

A decidedly efficient performance, she thought, and quite a change for Winterwalk. Laura's mother hadn't really been up to running a house this size, especially after her husband's defection, when her emotional condition, which had always been fragile, had truly begun to deteriorate. Laura remembered her childhood as a series of bland or burned meals served by surly maids, eaten alone at this same long table while her mother rested in the bedroom upstairs.

How different this was! Laura was impressed with how quickly Drew's cook had managed to provide for a surprise guest, though halfway through the chicken she realized that the food she ate probably had been intended for Ginger. The thought spoiled her appetite, and she lay her fork down slowly.

"Would you like to look around a little?" Drew took a last sip of coffee and, as he set his cup in the saucer, nodded at the maid, who hovered nearby, waiting to clear their plates. "It's been a while, and you might want to get reacquainted."

"Yes, thanks," Laura said, trying to sound enthusiastic. Reacquainted? She remembered every ostentatious square inch of this house, the way she might remember a particularly vivid nightmare. "That's probably a good idea."

"Let's start with the conservatory." Drew stood, tossing his napkin on the table. "It's the only thing I've changed much. The new gardener is a wizard. He's brought everything back to life, even some of the plants I'd given up on."

The conservatory. Laura mangled her napkin in her suddenly moist palm. She pictured it as she had last seen it—an eerie, abandoned place, an iron-domed Victorian vault of filthy, smudged glass and brown, withering twigs. A shiver ran over her skin.

But she should have known that Drew would try to revive that once lovely room. He'd always said it was criminal how Elizabeth Nolan neglected it. But Laura understood completely. Damian Nolan had used the conservatory as both studio and gallery, filling it with his sculptures and marking it indelibly with his presence. After he left, her mother had entered that room only when she absolutely had to—only, that is, on those nights when Laura walked in her sleep.

For some mysterious reason it had always been Laura's destination. Night after night she crept down to the dying conservatory, took off her clothes and knelt beside the pond that once had been full of water lilies, and she had cried, as if she wanted to replenish the pool with her tears.

But Drew couldn't have known that. He couldn't have guessed, as Laura followed him through the serpentine trail of rooms that led to the south wing, that her heart was knocking strangely, and she couldn't manage even a murmur in response to his polite small talk.

When they reached the door, Drew flung it open, standing back to allow Laura to enter first. For a minute she thought she wouldn't be able to do it. Her heart seemed to be pounding in her ears. Her head was light, and her feet felt numb, but she forced herself to walk, slowly, carefully, watching the ground, taking the black and white marble tiles one at a time, concentrating on not stepping on any of the cracks, like a kid playing a game. It seemed to help, a little.

"What do you think?" Drew put his hand lightly on the small of her back, and she was grateful for the balance it offered her dizzied world.

Slowly she looked up and, stunned, she caught her breath with a gasp. It was beautiful. It was green and lush and warm and wonderful—and for a fraction of a second she thought she could remember being happy here, happy and loved, long, long ago, before Damian had left them, before her mother's heart and spirit had been broken, before the decay had set in, killing the leaves and flowers, breeding contagion in the stagnant pool ...

She blinked. Had it ever really been like this? Had it ever felt so clear and clean and fresh? Or was this some magic Drew himself had worked, some glimpse she was getting of an Eden she would never know?

"Oh, Drew," she breathed, afraid to break the spell.

The pressure of his hand increased. "Like it?"

She almost said yes. She almost let herself believe that Drew had changed it, that he and his wizard gardener had been able to rid this place of its secret poison. But just then Drew shut the door behind them, and a current of air swam invisibly through the greenery, subtly agitating whatever it touched. Suddenly everything seemed alive, shifting, whispering.

And then she saw it. From behind the thick trunk of a twenty-five-foot *Monstera* plant, almost lost in the foliage, a white hand beckoned, palm up, its slender forefinger crooked enticingly. Laura's knees seemed to liquefy as her eyes sought the space, just slightly higher, where a white face peeked around the trunk, smiling knowingly, silently, urging Laura to come farther, deeper into the room's maze of trailing, twining vines.

Laura steadied herself against the back of an iron bench as she stared into the blind marble eyes, fighting a strange rush of nausea. "The statues," she said to Drew, her voice faint. "You've put them out again."

"Yes," he said, moving past Laura to pluck a dead leaf from the smiling statue's wrist. Laura shuddered, watching his strong golden fingers on that cold, pale skin. "I think I've got them in the right places. I wanted it to look just the way Damian designed it."

Drew sounded pleased, and as he surveyed the room
with an air of satisfaction, Laura forced herself to look
around. Was it exactly the same? Suddenly compelled
by the need to be sure, she moved into the center of the
conservatory, where she could, by turning slowly, see
all the statues.

She knew so well where to look. One little girl
crouched in the corner, frozen in an endless game of
hide-and-seek, her hand to her mouth as if smothering
a giggle ... or a scream. Another child, over in the ivy,
was even younger, almost a baby. He reached up with
both chubby hands, begging to be lifted free of the vines
that snaked around his bare feet and ankles.

Just beyond the bank of dragon's mouth orchids, the
lily pond shone like black glass. And there a girl raised
herself out of the water on slender marble arms—an
emerging mermaid, her back arched, her hair streaming across her naked torso.

Yes, they were all here, all the sweet, silent children
her father had sculpted. He had never sold any of his
work. Some people said, behind their hands, that he
didn't have to. He had married money, and now he
could indulge his hobby full-time, like the dilettante he
was. But Laura had known that he really loved his
work. She could almost see him now, hunched shirt-
less over the statues, his bare back sweating as he
rubbed over and over, roughly but rhythmically, at the
stone, polishing until it gleamed like smooth, wet ice.

Finally she forced herself to look to her right, where
a pedestal had once held the block of marble that
Damian Nolan had gouged and chipped and chiseled
until it looked just like his ten-year-old adopted
daughter. Her mother had banished the marble head to
the basement, along with the other sculptures, and the

pedestal had stood empty for fifteen years. But apparently Ginger had seen it, so Drew must have returned
it to its place of honor. Funny—she would have expected him to leave it in the basement, not wanting any
reminders of his faithless fiancée to mar the beauty of
this restored conservatory.

Without breathing, Laura lowered herself onto the
white iron love seat, staring at the sculpture, remembering the long hours she had sat there, on that same
cold bench, posing for her father.

It was like meeting a ghost of herself. The sculpture
had a strangely unfinished look. The eyes were by far
the most detailed feature, large and wide and clear and
brimming with sadness. The rest of the face was almost unformed, as if time had yet to decide whether she
would be firm of jaw, sensual of mouth. Only the sadness had been predetermined.

"Beautiful, isn't it?" Drew put two fingers under the
child's chin. "Damian was a very talented sculptor."

Her own chin tingled, and she lifted it, breathing
deeply.

"Did you ever think it was strange," she asked suddenly, sweeping an arc around the room with her gaze,
"that he sculpted only children?"

Drew tilted his head. "Strange?" He frowned at the
marble portrait of Laura. "How?"

She wound her fingers tightly together in her lap. She
and Drew had never agreed about Damian. Through
the years, Laura had always been deeply resentful,
blaming her father's desertion for the dramatic decline
of her mother's emotional stability and the ensuing
loneliness of her own life. Drew, on the other hand, had
admired the sculptor greatly and had more than once

suggested that her mother's eccentricities might have driven him away.

"Didn't you ever think..." She hesitated, wondering how she dared voice this terrible idea to Drew, who had been so fond of Damian. But surely it had occurred to him before. His older sister, Stephanie, had been the model for the mermaid. Look at the high, budding breasts of that statue, at the come-hither sensuality in the other statue's white, beckoning hand. "Did you ever think that perhaps his interest in children was—" her eyes finally met Drew's "—unhealthy?"

"What are you suggesting, Laura?" Drew withdrew his hand from the marble head as if it had suddenly burned his fingers. "Do you mean it might have been *sexual*?"

She nodded, the idea settling like a cold chunk of stone in the pit of her stomach.

"I'm saying perhaps he molested the little girls who posed for him," she said slowly, painfully aware of the implications. "I'm saying perhaps he molested me."

3

"Do you really believe that, Laura?"

Drew's skepticism couldn't be more obvious, though his voice was gentle, as if he was humoring a sweet, delusional great-aunt—reluctant to offend her, but loath to let her lose touch with reality completely. "That doesn't sound like Damian to me. Do you actually remember anything like that happening?"

"No," she admitted, shifting on the iron seat. "But perhaps I wouldn't. I mean, maybe it's a memory I've repressed." She saw his brows lift, and her voice tightened defensively. "It happens, Drew. The papers are full of it."

"Yes," he said mildly, "it's very much in vogue, I hear."

The implication stung, and she pressed her fingertips into the bench, trying not to grow angry. After all, he could be right. She didn't really *know* that any such horror had ever taken place. She was only guessing, trying to make the jagged pieces of her life fit together somehow.

"Actually, that psychiatrist you recommended so highly was quite fond of the theory," she said. "Every question he ever asked was leading me toward that conclusion. It's as if he assumed at the outset that I had been abused, and it was up to me to prove I hadn't been."

Drew frowned slightly, and she subsided, forcing herself to swallow the lump of self-pity that had risen in her throat. Whatever had or hadn't happened to her—none of it was Drew's fault. He was only trying to help. But he didn't understand, no one could, how terrifying it was to have these blank spots in her life, these nightly descents into the underworld of her soul. And it was even more frightening to know that, if she was ever going to understand what was happening to her, she had to do battle with all the hideous creatures that might be hiding there.

"I'm not saying it's impossible, Laura." Drew joined her on the bench, which was just barely wide enough for both of them. Instinctively she edged into her corner, but Drew settled comfortably, as if he didn't even notice the warm contact of their shoulders and thighs. "To be honest, I've thought of it before. It was certainly the most obvious answer for—" He broke off. "For everything. But if anyone hurt you, I don't believe it was Damian. I knew him well. He wasn't capable of doing anything so cruel."

Wasn't he? Laura stared at the sad marble eyes in front of her. Her own eyes. Hers was the last sculpture Damian Nolan had done. Had he known, even while he worked on it, that he was going to leave? Had the portrait been his goodbye gift?

"It was fairly cruel to abandon your wife and your ten-year-old daughter," she said dully.

"True." Drew sighed. "Cruel, but not *sick*. Not perverted. Hard as it was for you and your mother, Damian's not the first man to find his home life intolerable, is he?" He ran his palm down the corded fabric of his pants leg. "But we've been over this so many times,

Laura. You know your mother wasn't particularly easy to live with. They fought all the time—"

"I managed to live with her. I didn't run away." Laura stood, suddenly short of breath. She didn't want to talk about it anymore. "But you're right. We've been over this too many times, and we still need to deal with some practical things. We haven't even decided where I'll sleep tonight. I thought maybe the tower, if you have no objection. The tower room has only one door, and it would be easier for you to monitor...things."

But Drew wasn't about to be deflected. "Laura, listen to me," he said, leaning forward, his voice serious. "Isn't it possible that your problems are connected with your feelings of abandonment? Think about it. Maybe consciously you hated your father for running away, but maybe, on some subconscious level, you're still looking for him."

Laura shut her eyes, squeezed them, as if she could block his words from entering her consciousness. But still she remembered the nights she had walked in her sleep, always coming back to this spot, the place most intimately connected with her adopted father—the last place she had seen him.

"Think about it," Drew repeated, his voice low and intense. "Doesn't it make sense that, now that your mother is gone, those fears should resurface? That, in some primitive way, you feel left behind again?"

"I don't know," she said, her discomfort suddenly spiraling out of control. Her breath came quickly. "I don't know."

He stood now, as well, and their shoulders were once again only inches apart. "And isn't it possible," he said, "that fear of abandonment is responsible for your other problems, too?"

She jerked away, turning her back to him. "Don't be ridiculous," she said. She tried to breathe deeply, but her lungs seemed to be made of something stiff and unyielding. Perspiration beaded on her upper lip. She had to get out of here. It was too hot, the air too wet and warm and thick. The glass walls were weeping with condensation.

She cast her gaze around frantically. Even the mermaid appeared to be straining, struggling to escape from her watery prison. "Drew, I really don't want to talk about it anymore."

But he seemed not to have heard her. "Doesn't it make sense, Laura?" His deep tones were insistent. "Maybe you've always been afraid of intimacy, afraid to give too much to a man—a *lover*—for fear he'll leave you, too."

THEY DECIDED on the tower room. Or rather, Drew let Laura decide. She had been so distressed in the conservatory, so desperate to avoid his unwelcome words that she had practically fled from his side, her eyes wide and haunted, her skin as pale as the marble statues. Obviously his comments had struck a nerve.

After that, he hadn't had the heart to argue with her about anything. If she'd suggested sleeping in a pup tent in the backyard, he'd probably be driving stakes into the frozen ground right now. Luckily, her plan made sense. The tower bedroom, directly above his office suite, had only one window, which had long ago been barred, and only one door, which led into a small anteroom that would easily accommodate a cot for him.

They went to bed early, Laura pleading travel fatigue. While she showered in the downstairs bathroom, Drew stood in the doorway between the two small bedrooms, unbuttoning his shirt as he double-checked his housekeeper's arrangements.

As he could have predicted, Mrs. Rose had given Laura the first-rate, visiting-dignitary treatment. Her bed was swathed in pale blue silk sheets and piled high with thick, downy comforters to help combat the chill that permeated the tower in spite of Winterwalk's otherwise efficient central heating. Mrs. Rose had even brought up a pitcher of hot tea, a small cup warmer and several popular novels and magazines.

His own quarters were more spare, simply a cot set up along one wall, though he, too, got the silk sheets and soft blankets, he noted with an internal grin. Mrs. Rose was an incurable romantic. She'd also sent up a comfortable leather chair and put a week's worth of newspapers and a carafe of coffee on the adjoining end table. No one could have guessed that these rooms hadn't been used in fifty years. Drew made a mental note to give the lady a kiss and a raise.

"Oh, this is lovely!"

Drew turned, his shirt half free of his waistband. Laura stood in the doorway, dressed in a floor-length robe that was as softly swirling as blue wood smoke. Her face was dewy and pink from scrubbing, and she must have washed her hair; it was loose, tumbling over her shoulders, and the ends that curled just above her breasts looked slightly damp.

At the sight of her, something very male stirred deep inside him, but with an instinct perfected over too many miserable years, he clamped down on the urge mercilessly. He tugged the last edge of his shirt free, and shrugging out of it tossed it on the cot.

Get hold of yourself, Townsend. Surely he wasn't going to have to learn *that* lesson all over again! It was painfully simple. Any fool who allowed himself to desire Laura Nolan was as stupid as the greyhounds who chased plastic rabbits around in circles.

"Your housekeeper has worked a miracle up here," Laura said, smiling a shade too brightly, talking a bit too fast. She was a nervous wreck, Drew realized as he plopped on the edge of his cot to remove his shoes.

"Yeah." He spoke to the floor. "She's a gem." Shoes and socks off, he straightened. Now that he was down to his trousers, Laura's pink cheeks had drained to a bloodless alabaster, and she seemed to be having a hard time deciding where to look.

Grabbing his discarded clothes, he stood, holding back an annoyed oath. What the hell did she think he was going to do? Strip buck naked and make a diving lunge for her virginity after all this time? Hell, if he'd been going to lose control, it would have been back at nineteen, when he was six walking, talking feet of rampaging hormones. Or at twenty-two, when years of deprivation had made him a little crazy. Or at twenty-four, when he could see the woman he loved, the future he'd planned, slipping away from him. But not now. Damn sure not now.

She averted her eyes as he walked barefoot to the small half bath that was really no more than a glorified closet. He went inside, pulling the door shut, and began changing into a comfortable old pair of sweatpants. He'd be damned if he'd stay fully dressed, tossing and turning all night just because she didn't want to remember he actually had a body.

"Honestly, these rooms have never looked so cozy." Laura's voice was muffled. He could picture her, standing ramrod stiff, her back to the bathroom, even though it would take X-ray vision to see anything through the closed door. "They used to be a lot like prison cells, don't you think? I used to come up here all the time and play Rapunzel, wishing like mad that I really did have golden hair, like your sister."

He laughed, but as he came out of the bathroom, his sweatshirt in his hands, he saw that she had moved to the window and was staring down pensively, twirling a lock of hair around her index finger, as if she expected the wicked witch to be out there right now, demanding admittance. *Rapunzel, Rapunzel, let down your raven hair.*

He wasn't surprised Laura had chosen that fairy tale as her fantasy. After all, in a way it mirrored her life. Ever since she was ten years old, she'd been forced into a strange isolation with her embittered mother. Had Laura dreamed, even as a child, that someday a brave and clever prince would be able to penetrate her lonely prison, to climb up her thick, silken hair and rescue her?

And should he have done exactly that? Should he have ignored all her defenses and simply stormed the tower? Was she secretly disappointed that he hadn't? Well, God knows he'd wanted to. Remembering just how much he'd wanted to, his muscles tightened, mindlessly readying themselves for a battle he'd lost three years ago.

Enough! He clenched his teeth and flung his sweatshirt over the arm of the leather chair. *Sorry, Princess, it wasn't that easy,* he thought bitterly. *First you would have had to let down your hair.*

He walked to the window, hoping she couldn't sense his tension. "I used to come up here, too." He was at her elbow. "The year I was about eight. Your house was more interesting than mine, more like a real palace. I'd pretend I was king of the castle, lord of all I surveyed."

He looked down at the moon-white snow. "Pretty spectacular kingdom, don't you think?"

She nodded without speaking. Words really weren't necessary—the fairyland below them spoke for itself. The sky was a deep, thick purple, and light from the full moon caught on a thousand snow crystals. Ancient pines sparkled, giant Christmas trees decorated with spun sugar and diamonds. In the center of the front drive, glistening sprays of ice rose from the mouth of the frozen fountain like a magical flower.

They stood that way for a long minute, sixty seconds of silence during which Drew's focus shifted, against his will, from the wonderland below to Laura herself. He was close enough that her robe brushed against his bare chest, and his nostrils filled with the soft, peachy scent of her shampoo.

Without thinking, he took a deep breath. He knew that smell so well, knew how rich it was down in the deeper layers, next to her neck, where it mingled with the wildflower of her perfume. And he knew that somewhere in all that intoxicating sweetness was the elusive feminine scent of Laura herself. Night after night he had buried his face in her hair, breathing deeper, faster, trying to find it and hold it and make it a part of his blood.

He backed up a step, his head suddenly light. "Laura," he said, "why did you really come back here?" One step wasn't enough, so he took another, and mercifully the whisper of peaches faded. "You must have made friends in Boston. Wouldn't it have been simpler to ask one of them to help you?"

She didn't turn around. "Do you want to know the truth?"

The muscles in his abdomen seemed to draw in tightly. "Of course," he said. Did she think he couldn't take it?

"I almost did," she said. "But, you see, no one in Boston knows anything about where I come from." Reaching up, she gripped the window frame. "They think I'm just like everybody else, slaving for a pay-check, rooting for the Red Sox, looking for Mr. Right." Her hand tightened, the slim fingers curling around the ornately carved wood. "They would never understand all this—not the sleepwalking or the sculptures or this house or *any* of it."

When Drew didn't answer, she half turned her head, just enough to let him glimpse her profile. "And I don't want them to. That doesn't make any sense at all to you, does it, Drew?" she said defiantly. "But I like be-ing normal. When I go back, I want to be able to leave behind me whatever terrible things I may learn here. I don't ever want any of the people in my new life to look at me with pity or with morbid curiosity."

Her new life. Naturally he'd known she had one. But, hearing her speak of it so reverently, he felt unreason-ably angry. Her "old" life hadn't been all nightmares and repressed horrors. "It sounds a lot like running away."

At that she finally turned to face him. "You're damn right it does," she said, flushing. "I *hate* this house. I came back because I finally accepted it's the only way to be rid of the sleepwalking. But then I'm going to run like hell."

HE STAYED AWAKE for hours, lying on his narrow cot, listening through the open door to every small cough, every rustle and every sigh that came from Laura's room. Then, when there was only silence, he listened to that, too, his mind obsessively picturing how she must look while she slept, her hand under her cheek, her hair like black ribbons spread out along the blue pillowcase. It required all his willpower to keep himself from going in to see if reality matched his imagination.

In the end, though, he knew it would be an abuse of her trust, and chivalry carried the point. He tried to ignore the coiled tension in his muscles, the unrelieved heat that had gathered low in his body, but, damn it, he'd always known chivalry was criminally overrated.

When he finally slept, he dozed fitfully, dreaming strange, shamelessly symbolic dreams of melting towers and bloodied swords and flowers made of ice. He woke often, his heart pounding and his body aroused, and he groaned into his pillow. They'd better get to the heart of her sleepwalking soon. He couldn't take many more nights like this.

In the deep of the night, at the height of his dreams, he woke again, but this time he sensed he wasn't alone. Raising himself on one elbow, he rubbed the blur from his eyes and looked around. Laura stood by his window, her back to him, her head bowed, her body still.

"Laura?" He spoke from the cot, reluctant to rise. His sweatpants had been chosen for comfort, not for their ability to conceal. But she didn't turn around. "Are you all right?"

He stood, wishing suddenly that he had grilled her more thoroughly on the signs of her sleepwalking. She seemed to hear him come up behind her, for as he drew closer she turned slowly toward him, and he could see the play of moonlight on silver tears.

"Drew." Her voice was low, but she sounded perfectly normal. Did sleepwalkers talk? Could their gaze be so serious and clearly focused? Did they recognize the people around them and call them by name? Surely not. Drew's anxiety subsided. This wasn't compulsion—this was something much simpler. It was insomnia, fueled by loneliness and fear. He knew all about that.

"Yes, Laura," he answered. "I'm here."

She sighed, a deep exhale of relief that misted warmly against the wall of his chest. "Drew," she said again, inching even closer, as if she expected him to embrace her. He knew she needed comforting; she wanted someone to dry those silver tears. But he couldn't do it. He didn't trust himself to handle this confusing new role of guardian angel, not when his body was already thrumming with awareness.

"You were wrong," she said suddenly. The moonlight picked out soft glimmers in her eyes, and he could tell that her gaze focused somewhere around his chin, as if she didn't dare meet his eyes. "My father didn't want to abandon me. I know that."

Her father? A knife blade of shame sliced at his gut. So that was why she had been crying. How long had she been lying there, fretting about what he had said?

"Of course he didn't," Drew assured her, rushing his words as if he must hurry to erase the damage. He couldn't bear to think he had added to the weight that had already been crushing her. "Damian adored you. Everyone knew that. He wouldn't ever have left you if he could have seen any other way."

She didn't answer, her glistening gaze even lower now, somewhere near his collarbone. He wiped the dampness from her cheeks with gentle fingers.

"Next time why don't you just tell me to keep my big mouth shut?" He wished he could coax even a hint of a smile from her serious lips. Her smile was extraordinary, as most rare things were, full of light and beauty. "I may consider myself an authority on the stock market, but you could put everything I know about the subconscious in the palm of your hand." He lifted her left hand, holding it between them, palm up. He traced a circle on the soft skin. "And still have room to spare."

Her hand was so warm, like sun-kissed silk, and her slender fingers twitched subtly as he ran his thumb along the perimeter of her palm. He knew he ought to let go, but he couldn't. It had been a thousand starving days since he had last held her hand.

She sighed once, heavily, and then, still without looking into his eyes, she slowly placed the fingers of her other hand against the hollow at the base of his throat.

The movement caught him by surprise, and his pulse leaped in a hot, painful thrust. "Laura—"

"Oh, Drew," she whispered. Frozen in disbelief, he could only watch as she leaned forward, her dark cloud of hair cloaking her face, and pressed her lips softly against the throbbing pulse. Excitement leaped like a dagger of fire within him, even while his mind was saying no—this can't be happening—this can't be real.

But if it was a dream, it wasn't over yet. Boldly, as if she had been trained since puberty in some exotic art of seduction, Laura let her hand slide down his chest. She tunneled her fingers into the crisp dusting of hair, blindly nuzzling toward his nipples, which had hardened to nubs of delicious, painful sensitivity. She touched them, circled them with tiny butterfly strokes and then left them, aching tightly, to trace a long line of fire between his ribs.

"Laura, don't," he said, the syllables low and strangled, but as if she didn't hear him or didn't speak his language, her strokes didn't falter. He sucked in his breath on a growling hiss as her fingers kept going, down the clenched valley of his abdomen, and still farther, still down, down...

"For God's sake, Laura—" But her fingers were sure, unhurried, skimming over his waistband, sliding across the flimsy cotton, until with a sweet, wanton murmur of pure satisfaction, her hand finally closed around the rigid length of him.

He groaned low in his throat, his entire lower body tightening compulsively, as if electrified. He had come to her already half-aroused, but the maddening trail of anticipation she had just mapped across his skin had taken him to a level of frantic readiness he had never known before.

He wasn't sure he could stand it. He felt stretched to the screaming point, and he had a sudden fear that her touch alone might bring him to a shameful, wonderful, mind-bending climax right here, right now. He felt it starting already, coiling and twisting deep in his gut, and in some crazed corner of his mind he even wanted it. Wanted it fast. And hard. And *now*.

But no... this was all wrong. He didn't really want to do this, not like this. He fought for control, fought to hold back the blood that was already racing through him, struggled to quiet the muscles that had already begun to quiver in her palm.

No. He took her hand and stilled it, squeezing his eyes shut and letting his head fall back so that he could breathe deep, bracing gulps of air. No.

"Drew," she whispered again, plaintively. "I want you so much."

His heart skipped a beat, then thudded with a thick, slow, dreadful thrill. He had never heard her say that before. "I love you," she had said tenderly, desperately, even apologetically. But never "I want you." And she had never touched him like this.

"Laura, are you sure?" Was that his voice, that tight, fevered sound? "Oh, God, Laura, don't do this to me if you're not sure."

For answer, she took his free hand and placed it at the neckline of her robe, where the zipper's silver pull ring lay cold and flat under his fingertips. Though it was not what he had expected, her message was clear.

For one emotionally paralyzed moment he couldn't force himself to do it. What if this time was just like all the others, just another terrible, teasing torture, a rack on which to stretch and break his self-control?

She shifted, and the gentle swell of her breast grazed against the underside of his arm. Oh, God . . .

He held his breath, once again fighting for control, as he took the ring between his thumb and forefinger. He pulled it down slowly, trying to give her a moment to adjust to what was happening. Never before had he been able to unzip a single zipper, undo a single button, unhook a single clasp, without Laura clutching desperately at his hands, fighting, rejecting, begging him to stop.

Miraculously, this time there was no reaction at all, except perhaps a subtle quickening of her breath and the moist glistening of her lips as she ran her tongue across them.

"I'm going to take your robe off, Laura," he said in low, measured tones. It was torture to force the wild bolero beat of his blood into this tame, saraband pace, but he knew he had to try. "Nothing is going to happen unless you want it to. If anything I'm doing frightens you, just say so, and I'll stop."

He hoped that was true. He closed his eyes, dragged in a deep breath and prayed for the strength to make it true.

He slid his hand inside the robe, caressing the velvety mound of her shoulder as he eased the robe down her arm. Then the other side, an inch at a time. The robe caught briefly on her elbows, then fell to the floor in a whispering blue cascade.

A deep, unseen shudder shook him. "You're so beautiful, Laura," he whispered, wishing some other, more iridescent, magical word existed to describe the milky symmetry of her body as she stood in the cold winter moonlight.

"Let me see the rest of you," he said, running his finger along the lacy neckline of her gown, nudging the shoulder straps aside slowly, until they dangled around her upper arms, useless. The gown was made of a material so delicate that he could almost see the exquisite curves, the tantalizing swells and shadows, of her body beneath it. Almost. But almost was just another word for torture.

"Show me," he said, his voice thick. He could feel a faint vibration of her muscles, a shimmer of tension that told him she had, for the first time, grown taut, mutely wary. But she didn't resist as he pulled the soft material of her gown over the swell of her breasts, exposing her to the muted moonlight.

Oh, Laura . . . His knees liquefied as pure, undiluted hunger shot through him. He had imagined her, dreamed of her, longed for her, but never had any of the fantasy Lauras he created come anywhere close to the gut-wrenching beauty of the reality. He nearly doubled over with the need to touch her.

Still he struggled for control. He had to be prepared to stop whenever she asked him to, as he had promised. *Don't ask me, Laura,* he prayed silently. *Please don't ask me to stop.*

He slipped her arms free, one elbow at a time, then he dropped to his knees, gently tugging the gown around her hips, letting it fall alongside the abandoned robe.

He stopped, waiting, trying to slow his heart, to absorb the miracle that had come to him, trying to make himself understand that he really could touch her, taste her, learn her, own her. His body was suddenly racked with shivers, and he buried his face in the warmth of her stomach.

"Drew." Her voice was shaking, and the hand she placed on his shoulder trembled sharply. "I need you," she said, inhaling raggedly.

Swiftly, cursing his heartless self-absorption, he rose to his feet. She was pulsating with need—he could feel it in her neck, her throat, her temple—but that jagged sound of tears in her voice proved that she wasn't yet quite free of old chains.

"Don't be afraid," he said, taking her damp face between his hands, kissing where the tears had been. "It's going to be all right, Laura. I swear to you, this time it's going to be all right."

She wrapped her arms around his neck, pressing her quivering body against him, a slender, battered reed seeking shelter. Drew was suddenly filled with a sense of power, a thrill of certainty. The time for pulling back was past.

Scooping her into his arms, he carried her to the rumpled cot and lay her down, murmuring soothing sounds. He stepped back to shed his sweatpants, and in less than a heartbeat he stood before her, no longer able to conceal the evidence of his formidable desire.

"Look at me, Laura." But she wouldn't. He could see in her face the first flickerings of their old enemy—full-blown, paralyzing panic. He wouldn't let her give in to it. "Laura. Look at me."

Time slowed to an agonizing pace while he waited for her to obey. He knew that, to her softer, passive body, he must seem aggressively male, threateningly potent. But they had to get past this moment. She had to face the truth. All sex had an element of violence. She had to trust him, not because he couldn't hurt her, but because she knew he wouldn't. Slowly he sat beside her on the narrow cot.

"There's no need to be frightened. I'd never hurt you, Laura. You must know that." She didn't answer, but she opened her eyes, and the wildness had taken over even more of her. Gently, deliberately, he placed her hand on him again, though the nervous fluttering of her fingertips almost unmanned him.

"You know what this means, don't you, Laura? It doesn't mean power, and it doesn't mean pain. It means that I want you, that I want to be inside you, to be a part of you."

She moaned, her hand closing around him tightly. He shuddered, but hung on. "Our bodies are made this way for loving, Laura, not for hurting. There is a place inside you that is waiting for this. If you shut your eyes you can feel it." Her eyes drifted shut, her brows constricting as if in pain, and her pelvis shifted again restlessly.

Her hand moved, too, and Drew knew he had to hurry. He reached out slowly, brushing the dusky darkness between her legs with a feathered touch. "You want me, don't you, Laura?" A sweet heat guided his fingers easily to the tiny pinpoint of her desire, and he thumbed it softly. "Open for me, Laura. Let me come in and love you."

As if his voice, his touch, had hypnotized her, she let her legs fall apart with tantalizing grace, making a small, surrendering sound that seared along his flayed nerve endings like liquid fire.

He focused his attention on the swollen bud beneath his fingers, drawing small circles with his thumb and forefinger. Soon her head was tossing gently on the pillow, and thankfully her hand fell away from him as she reached up to clutch the sheets beside her head. She had forgotten fear, had apparently even forgotten him, lost in her mounting passion.

"Drew!" Her sudden cry was frantic, and she reached out blindly. She was almost beyond him now, arching painfully, caught in some black inner spiral of sensation.

It was time. He pulled away his hand and, poising himself over her, he finally allowed the moment of truth to arrive. If she rejected him now, there was nothing more he could do. . . .

It was the sweetest, most excruciatingly painful moment of his life. He entered her gently, lowering his lips at the same moment to the pebbled peak of her breast. She cried out, digging her hands into his hair, arcing under him with an uncontrollable passion.

He groaned with a relief that shimmered through his veins like a dawning. She tasted like midnight nectar, and she felt as warm as heaven, throbbing around him tightly but welcoming him, wanting him, needing him as much as he needed her.

He thrust slowly past the barrier of her maidenhead, hating that he had to hurt her, gathering her up against his chest to ease the momentary burning. She sobbed, tightening, and it was strangely as if her pain was his pain, too. A tear fell on his shoulder, and his own eyes grew wet. But then her tension eased, and with his hands under her hips, he completed the joining with a lover's long, deep, infinitely gentle stroke. It was done. She was his.

He couldn't tell the precise moment when they lost control, but suddenly her hips were writhing wildly under his, and her fingers dug into his hips, begging, demanding, controlling. He felt her begin to shatter, untutored muscles contracting helplessly, rhythmically around him, and he knew he couldn't wait any longer.

And then, with joy and pain and love and a thousand drowning emotions he didn't even have names for, he exploded, pouring into her every ounce of aching need he had stored for all these years inside his broken heart.

WHEN HE AWOKE, she was gone. For a horrible, heart-stopping moment he thought it had all been another dream. Through the years, he had actually imagined things almost as real as this had been. . . .

Then he saw the tiny red stain on his sheets, and the fist of fear relaxed its hold on his chest. It had been real. It had happened. He had found Laura last night, his Laura, the real Laura. And this morning all the world was different.

He rose, pulling on the sweatpants he must have kicked under the cot, and covered the stain with the sheets. She might well be self-conscious this morning, still confused, perhaps, by last night's encounter. No need to confront her with this intimate proof before they had time to talk, to get comfortable with one another again. It had, after all, been three long years.

But suddenly, before he could pull on his sweatshirt, she appeared in the doorway, fully dressed, a cup of coffee in her hands and a tense, false smile on her lips.

"Oh, Drew, good. I'm glad you're up," she said politely, and a shadow of déjà vu fell briefly over his spirits. This was exactly how she had sounded last night before they went to bed—friendly but superficial, bright chatter covering tightly strung nerves.

"You should have warned me what a sound sleeper you are," she said, refusing to meet his eyes, just as she had done last night. She smoothed her skirt and adjusted her belt. "That could be a problem, couldn't it, I mean, if you don't wake up when I start walking in my sleep?"

She tried to smile, but it was a dismal failure. "I think maybe I'm going to have to wear bells, or rig an alarm or something. Otherwise I'll be wandering all over Winterwalk without you ever knowing it."

Drew frowned. What the hell was she talking about? His instincts prickled. Something was wrong here. Sickeningly wrong.

She flushed under his scowling scrutiny, but the bright, impersonal voice stumbled on. "I'm pretty sure I walked again last night. I found my nightgown near the doorway between our rooms." She took a sip of her coffee, glancing at him over the rim of the cup. She seemed to be waiting for him to jump in with explanations.

But he didn't speak. He couldn't. He stalled, tugging his sweatshirt over his head while he tried to sort out what her oblique comments really meant. She wasn't quite making sense. He didn't dare speak, not until she made it clear what she felt about last night.

What she felt? That was hardly the main issue right now, was it? He forced himself to face the truly frightening implications of what she was saying. He couldn't be sure, what she even *remembered* about last night.

"It's rather awkward," she went on. "I don't know if I ever got as far as the conservatory. Maybe sleeping up here instead of in my old bedroom confused me." She grimaced in a misguided, miserable attempt at levity. "But you don't make much of a guard dog, do you? Apparently you slept through the whole thing."

4

SHE DIDN'T REMEMBER.

Drew was glad he was sitting down. A rather horrible burning feeling seemed to be sinking through his body, pooling in his suddenly weak legs. He stared at Laura's flushed cheeks, at her anxious eyes that were mutely begging for reassurance that she hadn't made a fool of herself last night. His chest tightened. This was impossible, unendurable, insane. But it was true nonetheless. He could see it in her eyes. She really didn't remember.

"It's so embarrassing," she rushed on when he didn't answer. "I probably spent half the night on the floor next to your bed. Although...who knows? I could have been dancing the hula on the roof." She tried to laugh, but the sound came out more like a choking sob. She set the coffee down on the end table, rattling the cup against the saucer as her fingers trembled slightly but talking all the while.

"Oh, it's just too ridiculous, isn't it, having a problem like this? It's like being two people, as if there's another me who wanders around at night doing God knows what." She shook her head helplessly and, sagging, propped herself against the wall. "And I can't control this other me. I don't even know her." She turned her begging gaze to Drew. "You can see what I'm up against, can't you? I wasn't exaggerating when I said I needed someone I could trust."

Trust. Suddenly Drew couldn't look at her, and he focused intently on tying his jogging shoes, though his fingers felt as rubbery and uncontrollable as elastic bands. Someone she could trust. He tried desperately to remember how she had looked last night, what she had said, but her words kept echoing hollowly in his ears, making thought difficult. Trust, trust, trust, the word was repeated, a battering ram against his brain. She needed someone who wouldn't take advantage of her nakedness, her helplessness.

Oh, God. He yanked the laces so tightly his foot throbbed, as the horror of it finally sank in. He had made love to a woman who had been, for all practical purposes, asleep. But he hadn't known, some remnant of self-defense cried thinly, rationalizing. She had seemed normal. She had spoken to him, looked at him, touched him . . .

Sudden self-loathing washed over him like nausea, and he smothered the pitiful excuses into silence. What he had done was indefensible, an act of ultimate treachery. He *should* have known. There must have been signs—signs that, in his rush toward gratification, he had ignored. The soft monotone of her voice, repeating his name over and over, almost hypnotically. The bold, uninhibited desire in her fingers. Her strangely passive submission as he removed her gown. And then, later, the confused, wild, unfocused stare he had believed was the product of passion.

His heart sped, sending a new stream of hot shame through his veins. God, yes—the signs had been everywhere. He should have realized instantly that Laura would never have done any of those things. Laura, who had always panicked, choking on her fear, whenever he had tried to touch her. Could he honestly have believed she'd suddenly turned into a hot-blooded siren?

But he had believed it. God help him, he *had.* That was, perhaps, the most damning evidence of all. Driven by lust, he hadn't even suspected that she might not be fully conscious. He had needed so badly to believe she really wanted him, that she was finally ready to return his love, that he had blinded himself completely to the truth.

"Laura," he began, still staring at his shoes. How could he say this? She would never forgive him. "Laura, listen—"

But abruptly she sank onto her knees beside him, her warm palms resting on his thigh, burning through his sweatpants, just as her hand had done last night. The muscles in his leg contracted painfully.

"Drew, I can't tell you how much I appreciate your help. I know you didn't want to do this." Her hands tightened, and, the words dying in his throat, he looked up. Her eyes were smoky and dark, full of an open vulnerability that made his stomach lurch. "I know I didn't really even have any right to ask you. But coming home has been very hard for me. Even harder than I imagined it would be. I honestly don't think I could go through with it if I didn't know you were the one...the one watching me. Protecting me."

He groaned deep in his throat. "Christ, Laura."

"No, let me say it. It's important. I know you have other women in your life now, Drew. Women who, well, who might not understand why your ex-fiancée is sleeping in your upstairs bedroom." She smiled bravely, but she swallowed hard, and her fingers quivered slightly against his tense, aching muscles. "So I wanted you to know I'll try hard to sort things out as quickly as possible. I've got two weeks' vacation. If I haven't made any progress in that time, I promise I'll go on back to Boston and leave you in peace. Does that sound fair?"

Fair? His vocal cords felt paralyzed. Who was he to say what was fair? His moral barometer was obviously profoundly off kilter.

As she watched his face, her smile faded, her eyes darkening. "One week, then? I know it's a lot to ask, but . . ."

He stirred restlessly. "Two weeks is fine." He stood, and her hand fell away from his thigh. Leaving her kneeling by the cot, he moved to the window and looked down at the gleaming landscape. "But do you think you're being realistic, Laura? Do you really think you can undo fifteen years of damage in two weeks?"

He heard her dress rustle as she stood. "I hope so," she said slowly. "I know it sounds naive, but I really think maybe I can. It's strange—ever since my mother died it's been as if something inside me is trying to get free, as if maybe the things I've repressed all these years are struggling toward the surface. I especially sense it here. It doesn't exactly feel good—in fact, it's downright scary. But for the first time in a long time, I feel something like hope." She hesitated. "Can you understand that?"

He nodded slowly, his heart sinking like a hot anchor in his chest. He understood, and because he did, he suddenly saw how impossible it would be to tell her the truth about last night, even if he wanted to. If his shame wasn't enough to keep him silent, his concern for her certainly would be. He realized that knowing what she was capable of doing in her dreamlike states would only create new fears for her, new demons to people her nightmares. She would be terrified of him, and even more destructively, of herself. Her newfound hope, this fragile self-confidence she had attained, could be blown to bits.

So it was going to have to remain his guilty, corrosive secret. The bittersweet relief of confession, with its hope of forgiveness, was not possible for him now. He would simply have to forget it had happened. And it hadn't, really, not the way he'd believed. It might just as well have been some other woman, some stranger....

His eyes burned suddenly, and he narrowed them against the pain, focusing hard on the scene below him. It must have snowed again just before dawn. The boughs of the pines drooped under their heavy burden, and the patio was carpeted in unbroken white, all traces of yesterday's footprints erased.

Even the weather had conspired to wipe the slate clean, he thought with a sudden surge of anger. He felt strangely betrayed, though he knew any objective judge would count *him* the betrayer. But, damn it, something important had happened last night, something miraculous, something he had thought they could build a future on. And now it was as if it never existed. It had no power to change his life, or hers. It had become, in essence, just another dream. A particularly vivid, painful dream that would haunt him forever.

LAURA spent the morning in the attic, praying for a miracle. But all she found was opulent debris collected by four generations of a family that had always been wealthy enough to indulge every acquisitive whim: simpering portraits framed in rococo gold; crate upon crate of ringing crystal goblets; ancient Chinese lacquered screens; huge mahogany tables that stood on

legs of fantastically carved fruits and animals; count-
less porcelain shepherdesses and lacy ladies who,
though priceless, had fallen out of favor.

Stuff. So much stuff. Squatting in front of an old
steamer trunk, Laura leaned back on her heels and
sighed, her breath condensing in the cold attic air, disappointment made visible. She felt no sense of life up
here, no connection with the people who had bought
these treasures. Was her family story really written in
money, a saga of the wallet instead of the heart? Was it
only on television the heroine finds a secret drawer in
the trunk that, when sprung, reveals a musty diary
filled with exclamation points and faded roses?

Not in these trunks. Half a dozen of them sat,
hunched and dusty, around the attic, and most of them
were filled with beautiful old clothes, ivory satins and
moonbeam beads, ostrich feathers and soft ecru lace.
They still held the scent of expensive French perfumes,
which rose from the rainbowed fabrics like silent music. But she'd already known that her family was rich.
And this was the last trunk, her last chance.

Refusing to give up, she buried her hands deeper into
the cool, slithering silks, all the way up to the elbows,
feeling for something else. Something...different.
Something ugly that didn't belong with all this beauty.
She didn't know what it was, but she knew without
question that such an ugliness had existed, that a poi-
sonous weed had once lurked somewhere in these
flowers.

Suddenly something sharp stabbed her finger. With
a low, shocked cry, she withdrew her hand quickly. At
first she thought it must have been an insect, a spider
perhaps, cross at being disturbed, but she saw immediately that she'd been cut. A teardrop of bright red

blood had already formed on the pad of her index finger and, before she could catch it, spilled onto the pristine white satin negligee that lay on top of the stack of clothes. For a minute she just stared in stunned indignation at the fabrics, overflowing the trunk as soft and frothy as pastel foam. What on earth?

Sucking on her throbbing finger, ignoring the slightly metallic taste of her blood, she sifted gingerly through the clothes with her other hand. She peeled back layer after layer of fabric, and then she found it. A long, pointed sliver of broken glass that curved like a scythe around the small plastic figure of a ballerina.

Laura recognized it immediately. Long ago, it had been her favorite possession—long, long ago, in a time that had been so innocent it almost seemed like a book she'd once read. All the glass was gone now—all but this last, lethal shard—but once it had been a magical snow globe. This little ballerina, arms gracefully arched above her head, had twirled amid a soft rain of floating, twinkling glitter. Laura turned the key now, winding the music box until it would turn no more, and then, holding her breath, she flipped the lever.

Miraculously, though her protective globe was shattered, the ballerina danced. A Tchaikovsky waltz filled the attic, the tinny plink of the steel teeth against the rotating cylinder imparting a particularly plaintive quality to the sweet, sad melody.

Listening, Laura was suddenly washed by a warm gush of memory. She had adored dancing once, hadn't she? At seven, eight or so, she had lived for her weekly ballet lesson, disobediently sneaking into her precious silver tutu whenever she could. She had loved to show off for her father, delighted when he had laughingly agreed to partner her, spinning her until she was dizzy or lifting her above his head like a soaring swan.

How could she have forgotten? She stumbled to her feet, rewinding the stem, lost in the memories. She had forgotten how graceful she'd felt, how comfortable and free in her body, and remembering was somehow like receiving a gift. She began to sway, letting the music soak into her. Official ballet steps were long lost, but she didn't care. She shut her eyes and let the dips and swells of the song tell her how to move. Her skirt swirled around her thighs, and her hair stung her neck as she danced, sublimely ignoring the awkward clutter, elevated above such mundane considerations by a feeling of complete sensual abandon.

When the box wound down, she opened her eyes slowly, reluctant to return to reality. She had waltzed into the corner of the attic, where an abandoned cheval mirror was tucked under one heavy beam. The woman she saw there shocked her—she was flushed, soft, pliant, lit with an inner joy.

And then, with a gasp, she saw his reflection. Tall and shadowed, little more than a dark ghost, standing in the attic doorway, watching . . .

She spun around, frightened, her hand at her throat, where a pulse beat frantically. How long had he been there? How much had he seen?

"Don't stop," Drew said, his voice deep in the silence. "It's beautiful."

She shook her head, feeling her flush intensify. She waved her hand vaguely toward the silent ballerina. "Oh, no, really. It's just—" she had to take a deep breath "—just something silly. . . ."

"It's not silly." Drew crossed the attic with purposeful strides and picked up the music box. With two deft fingers he twisted the stem, fast and hard, releasing stray, tinkling notes like champagne bubbles into the air. "It's beautiful," he said again. His eyes were very dark. "Dance for me, Laura."

And then he set it down. Laura watched, hypnotized, as the ballerina began her twirling and the melody floated out into the room. She couldn't move. She couldn't even look at him.

"Laura." Drew came closer and, slowly wrapping his arms around her waist, he subtly began to sway, moving so gently that she couldn't really be sure he *was* moving. It might have been her blood, which throbbed so hard in her veins that it seemed to rock her whole body. "Dance with me," he whispered, his breath warm against her ear, his palms nudging the curves of her hips.

How could she resist? He hadn't held her like this in so long, and yet his touch was so familiar. It was like coming home, but to a better, safer home than she had ever known. Her hands drifted to his shoulders, her head to his chest, as her body picked up the almost imperceptible rhythms, and then, once again, she gave herself over to the sensuality of the music.

They didn't speak. It was as unreal, as wonderful, as being locked in their own magical snow globe. Currents of cold, damp air eddied around their swaying bodies, and dust motes swirled like glitter in the pale shaft of winter sunlight that angled in through the window. In the mirror their reflections danced, too, dim and gray, as if the ghosts of their younger selves had joined them here.

They danced long after the music stopped, after the ballerina had once again stilled. But finally the spell that held them ended, and they slowed and pulled apart, suddenly self-conscious. Drew cleared his throat, and Laura ran her fingers through her mussed hair awkwardly, neither looking quite directly at the other.

Drew spoke first. "We've never danced before, have we?" He sounded surprised.

Laura shook her head. "No, I don't think so." She wasn't surprised, though. Dancing was just one of many lovely, intimate things they had never done together. Suddenly she saw how much youth and pleasure they had wasted with their desperate wrangling over sex.

He was looking at her, his eyes dark. "You dance very well."

She flushed again, knowing that he must be referring to her solo exhibition earlier. What they had just done together was too subtle to give him any hint of her talent. "Thanks," she said uncomfortably. "I used to love it—my dream was to become a prima ballerina, I think."

Drew ran his finger carefully along the long arc of broken glass, and Laura saw for the first time how it seemed to be pointing at the ballerina's heart. She shivered, and glancing at the window, realized it had begun to snow again.

"What happened to it?" he asked, resting the tip of his finger on the sharp point, testing it.

She frowned. "My dream? Or the music box?"

"Either." He looked up, his face in shadows. "Both."

The shiver ran through her again, stronger this time, and she folded her arms across her chest. Staring at the ballerina, she felt a strange sensation, a tugging, tightening feeling under her ribs. And then, as if it had been pulled from the depths of her unconscious, a half-formed memory appeared.

"My mother happened to it," she said, disconcerted, watching the memory take shape even as she spoke. "I think she didn't like my dancing." A disagreeable heat suffused her as the memory became clearer, took on color and sound. "She particularly didn't like me dancing with Damian. She had told me not to do it." She gazed at the sliver of glass. "When she caught me, she threw my music box down in a fury."

And now, with a painful clarity, Laura remembered, too, how she'd felt when her mother had dashed the beautiful globe to the ground. Angry. Bereft. Brokenhearted. And yet, beneath all those normal emotions, there had burned a shame, a humiliation that she had been caught doing something so wicked it needed to be punished so cruelly.

"How did Damian feel about that?"

She shook her head, squinting as if peering into a foggy distance. "I don't know," she said slowly. "I can't remember that part. I didn't remember any of it, actually, until I found the music box today."

She turned toward him, suddenly almost eager as she began to piece together the implications of her revelations. If she had forgotten that she had ever taken ballet lessons, wasn't it possible she had forgotten other things, as well? Surely Drew would be less skeptical about repressed memories now.

"You know, this may be important somehow, Drew," she said, seeing in her mind's eye her mother's anguished face as she picked up the shards of glass while Laura wept in the corner. Looking back, Laura could feel that the whole situation had been fraught with a level of emotional tension that was way out of proportion.

"It's a memory I've repressed for years. That alone may be significant. I honestly had forgotten that I ever took ballet lessons. Don't you think that for me to remember it now must mean—" She paused, trying to express herself accurately. "I don't know, really—it just feels like it means something."

Drew didn't look convinced. "What, though? Ballet lessons? A broken toy? It's not much to go on."

"Well," she said defensively, though she hadn't sorted it through completely yet, "don't you think it might mean that my mother already suspected there was something wrong with Damian, that she was afraid for me? Maybe that was why she didn't want him to dance with me."

Drew's brow knitted. "Don't you think you may be jumping to conclusions, Laura? Forcing every tiny fact you come across into proof of this preconceived theory of yours? Frankly, I think it's a hell of a leap from a broken music box to child abuse."

"The connection seems pretty clear to me." Laura was obscurely resentful, as if Drew was deliberately trying to sabotage her efforts to remember. "I know you were fond of Damian, Drew, but that doesn't necessarily mean I'm wrong. He could have—" she stumbled, looking for the right word, one that wouldn't sound hysterical "—hurt me."

To her surprise, Drew looked almost angry. "What exactly are you getting at, Laura? Look, we'd better be straightforward here if we ever expect to make any progress. Just say it. Do you think he *raped* you? Is that what you think?"

She raised her chin, stung by the harshness in his tone. "It's possible, Drew. Something has made me this way about sex, you know. It's *possible*."

"No, it isn't." Drew's brows were a straight dark line, hooding his eyes, and his hands were balled into fists at his side. "It isn't possible that he raped you, Laura."

Foolish tears stung at her eyes. "You don't know that."

He made an odd sound, a half laugh that turned strangely to a hiss at the end, as if he exhaled through clamped teeth. "Yes, I do," he said roughly.

"How?" Now she was angry, too. What arrogance! "Because he was such a *nice* guy? I hate to disillusion you, Drew, but every time they catch a mass murderer there's a neighbor who just can't believe it, because he seemed like such a *nice* guy." She hated the strident sarcasm in her voice but she couldn't stop herself. She knew if she could see her reflection in the cheval mirror now, it would look very different from that softly smiling girl she'd seen just minutes ago.

Drew's mouth tightened, and some extreme emotion seemed to possess his face, hardening the edges, deepening the shadows. Laura's anger abated briefly while she wondered what the emotion was.

She wished she could believe he hated the thought of anyone abusing a child, but he seemed too certain, too adamant that nothing of the sort had ever happened. Such a certainty was mystifying, to say the least. Drew couldn't have been more than twelve or thirteen at the time, hardly in a position to be completely sure that the man next door wasn't a monster in disguise.

No, more likely Drew merely found it objectionable for her to make accusations she couldn't prove. Or perhaps, since he had obviously grown so used to the fawning adoration of Ginger, he disliked Laura's implication that he was not an infallible judge of character.

"What about Stephanie?" he asked suddenly, his face relaxing slightly, as if he had finally found the compelling argument that would end the debate once and for all.

"Stephanie?" Laura was too emotionally exhausted to follow his logic. This was the way it had always been when they talked about this—at least this was how it had become by the end of their relationship, right before Laura and her mother had run away. She and Drew had tried to discuss their problems rationally, but they had both been too raw, too wretched and desperate after so many years of dashed hopes. The discussion had always degenerated into a quarrel, each of them feeling that the other simply didn't understand, wouldn't even try to understand. "What about Stephanie?"

"She posed for Damian, too," he said, with the triumphant air of a magician pulling a rabbit out of a hat. "And you have to admit you'd go a long way to find a healthier emotional specimen than Stephanie. She and Mark have been married eight years now, and they still hang all over each other like teenagers. They've got four kids running around Springfields. The fifth is due in a couple of months."

For a minute Laura didn't answer, feeling strangely deflated. Though it was hardly conclusive, Drew did have a point. Stephanie, Drew's older sister had been a stunningly beautiful teenager, and Damian had loved to work with her. He had carved several enchanting pieces for which Stephanie had been the model, but his finest creation had been the mermaid. Stephanie had happily posed day after day for weeks for that statue, never complaining about having to wear a clinging wet bathing suit, never fussing that the water was too cold.

Laura saw immediately what Drew meant. Surely if Damian Nolan had been driven by this terrible compulsion, a perverted need so irresistible that he would violate his adopted daughter, he wouldn't have been able to resist Stephanie. And yet obviously Stephanie didn't have an ounce of ambivalence about her own sexuality—no ghosts of childhood horrors haunted her marriage bed. Laura thought of the four beautiful children who now ran up and down the graceful halls of Springfields, children who might well resemble their uncle Drew, fair-haired and hazel-eyed.

What if they came to Winterwalk while she was here? Stephanie and Drew were very close. Surely the children would want to visit their uncle Drew. Could she stand seeing them, knowing they represented all that she had missed in life? Squeezing her eyes shut, Laura pressed her hands to either side of her head, as if the mental pictures were a physical pain. Why? Why was everything so easy for some people—so impossibly twisted for her? It wasn't fair, she cried inside, like a child. It simply wasn't fair. She, too, would have liked to have children, beautiful, laughing, healthy children with the Townsend smile.

"Why?" she finally said aloud, her voice pinched and tight from the effort to hold back her misery. She met Drew's hooded gaze, and finally her thwarted, childish frustration seemed to find a target. "Damn it, Drew, why are you so determined to dissuade me? Don't you want me to remember what really happened? Don't you *want* me to be able to get on with my life?"

"Of course I do!" Drew jerked away from her, and again the vehemence in his voice surprised her. He paced toward the open steamer trunk, and glaring at it, slammed it shut with his foot. The lid fell in place with a thump, sending the dust motes scattering in terror. "Of course I want you to remember, if you want to—if you can bear to." He dragged in a deep breath and pitched his voice lower. "But I just don't think you're ever going to get at the truth this way. I think you've written the whole scenario out ahead of time, according to some pop psychology theory that you find plausible. And I think you're trying to force the pieces of memory to fit into that theory whether they really do or not."

He spread his hands, then made frustrated fists in the air, grabbing and crushing some invisible adversary. "Don't you see the folly of it, Laura? You're going to be so busy trying to prove that prefab idea that you wouldn't know the truth if it bit you!"

Somewhere downstairs a door slammed shut, and the vibration jostled the music box just enough to coax one last, pitiful note from it. The high, strange sound hung in the thickened air for several seconds and then was supplanted by Ginger's throaty tones.

"Drew," she called. She made it a two-syllable word.

He didn't answer. He and Laura locked gazes, each standing military stiff, two soldiers in a silent war that had been going on far too long. Neither of them blinked.

Then Laura heard the distant whine of the elevator, descending in answer to Ginger's impatient finger on the button, no doubt. She'd be up here soon, Laura would bet on that. Ginger's female instincts were too good to leave Drew alone with his ex-fiancée for long.

"I know what you're trying to tell me," Laura said finally, forcing herself to maintain the unsettling eye contact. "I think you're wrong, but I can only promise I'll try to keep an open mind."

He didn't answer her, either. After a couple of seconds, she turned and headed for the door, but paused there, unable to resist one last shot.

"If it turns out I'm right, though, you'll regret some of the things you've said, Drew. You know you will."

His face looked strange in the muted light, and he shook his head slowly. "If it turns out you're right, Laura, if Damian—or *anyone*—took your virginity away from you thirteen years ago, I swear to God I'll be looking for a good psychiatrist myself."

ACTUALLY, Drew thought later as he and Ginger were working, or trying to work, on the stock tables, that psychiatrist thing might not be such a bad idea anyway. He could damn sure use some levelheaded, professional advice on what to do now. When he accepted this crazy guard dog assignment, his intentions had been so honorable, and look how thoroughly he'd botched things already.

He sighed heavily, the numbers in front of him drifting in and out of focus. It was as if he couldn't think straight anymore. He knew what he wanted to do. He wanted to take Laura into his arms and tell her the truth. He wanted to hold her and pet her and lead her back to the tower, to that narrow, waiting cot.

He had almost done it this morning, when they'd danced to that foolish music box in the attic. For just a minute, she had felt so warm, so...receptive. But then the music had ended, and she had pulled away, the warmth dying, her face closing like a locked door, presenting the blank, unreachable expression he remembered so well from the past. Seeing it, he'd known she was lost to him, so determined not to feel anything that she had almost mystically removed her emotions to some other plane, though her body still stood in front of him.

It was for the best, he had decided bitterly, looking at her empty face. To be brutally honest, he just didn't have the heart to start the whole pointless, eviscerating battle over again. He was through with Laura Nolan, thank God, through with all her hang-ups.

It was just that the emotional back-and-forth was making him crazy. It was turning him into this bossy, bullheaded jerk who couldn't even have a normal conversation with her without losing his temper. He'd gone up there to tell her lunch was ready, and he'd ended up in her face, barking that all her theories were worthless gibberish, all her efforts in vain. He'd practically had her in tears, for God's sake.

But damn it, he knew she was wrong. He *knew*. No man had ever had sex with Laura Nolan before last night, and he had the memories to prove it. Of course there were other violations, atrocities that wouldn't necessarily involve taking her virginity. . . .

"Excuse me, dear Mr. Townsend, sir." Breaking into his thoughts, Ginger's tap on his arm was insistent, her drawl playfully incredulous. "Did you really just say you want to invest in the Queen Serena Psychic Institute?"

Drew looked at her guiltily. His dark thoughts had taken him so far down such twisted mental corridors that he hadn't even realized she'd asked him anything. "Of course not."

"You did, too," she said, smiling to take the sting out of her contradiction. "I just mentioned that the Queen Serena Psychic Institute seems to have made a bundle

last year and maybe we should put some money in it."
She shoved a stack of files out of the way and wriggled
her bottom more comfortably on the edge of the desk.
"And you distinctly nodded. Vigorously, in fact."

"Sorry." He rubbed his eyes and tried to smile at her.
"I guess my mind was somewhere else."

"Mars, maybe?" She shook her head, despairing of
him. "This is getting to be a habit, you know."

"Sorry," he said again, shutting his eyes and dropping his head against the back of his chair. He was just
too tired to keep up with her incessantly playful rep-
artee. He hadn't had much sleep last night, although of
course he couldn't tell Ginger that.

Suddenly he felt her long, cool fingers take hold of
his hand. She pressed his palm against the silky curve
of her upper thigh. The hem of her skirt draped over his
knuckles, hiding his fingers, and under his hand he felt
the heat of her leg through the fine, tight mesh of her
expensive stockings. She wriggled an inch or two closer
to him, murmuring something soft and unintelligible.

The invitation, however, was crystal clear, and Drew
was shocked to discover it held absolutely no allure for
him. He kept his hand still, working through the implications of that discovery before he did anything
precipitate. What the hell was going on here? Why
should he suddenly feel squeamish about his relationship with Ginger? Last night with Laura had meant
nothing. Nothing. Hadn't he accepted this morning that
the whole insane thing would have to be forgotten,
buried like yesterday's footprints in the snow? Hell, it
might as well be a dream.

And even if this homegrown trauma therapy somehow miraculously worked, if Laura did manage to un-
kink her sexual knots, there was no reason to believe

she would want to come back to Drew. When she was awake and aware, she didn't even seem to like him very much. For all he knew, there was some doctor-lawyer-Indian-chief back in Boston waiting for her. Perhaps that waiting man was the real reason for her pilgrimage to Winterwalk.

But even as he listed all the reasons he'd be crazy to break up with Ginger now, Drew felt himself pulling his hand free. Gently, so that it didn't feel quite like a rejection. But firmly, so that there was no doubt. Because suddenly there was no doubt, not in Drew's mind. It might be insane—it might be self-destructive. But it was inescapable. He might never have Laura again but, having had her once, he could never settle for what he felt for Ginger.

Ginger knew instantly what his decision meant. Drew could see it in the brief narrowing of her eyes. But she was slick, he had to give her that. She carved another smile onto her lips and began to talk, her voice as full of syrup and sensuality as ever.

"You know," she said, easing off the desk with a kittenish stretch of her long, lovely legs, "I'm so tired of all this snow I could just about scream, aren't you? I could really use about a month in the tropics." She moved to the window, presenting her undeniably attractive backside to Drew for inspection. "You don't know of anyone in our Bali office who could use a topnotch administrative assistant, do you?"

He had to smile. "We don't have a Bali office."

She tossed a grin over her shoulder, half-hidden by her long blond hair. "We should get one."

"We have one in Miami, though," he said. "And I hear the administrative assistant down there is going on maternity leave soon." For a minute Drew marveled at the fortuitous coincidence, and then, when Ginger's smile broadened, he wondered whether she'd known this already. Was it possible she always kept Plan B in the back of her mind, ready just in case?

"Miami. Hmm." She sighed softly, "I was thinking maybe I'd be more useful in the L.A. office. I hear the director down there has just gone through a nasty divorce, and he probably needs someone with lots of experience."

The L.A. office. George Bradshaw. Drew dredged his mind for a picture of George. Thirtyish, good-looking, rich. Newly single. Ah... Drew felt himself being neatly maneuvered into place, slid across the chessboard of Ginger's life with one smooth, masterful nudge. But he didn't resist. The businessman in him couldn't help admiring her craft, and the jilting lover in him knew he owed her at least this much.

"Any idea," he asked, a quizzical smile on his face, "what I should do with the assistant who's already working in the L.A. office?"

Ginger turned around, meeting his grin. "Linda Denton. Well, let's see. Linda's got family in Miami," she said with a hint of a flourish in her voice. "She'd be glad to take over for the departing mommy-to-be in the Miami office."

Drew laughed and leaned back in his chair. "Tell me something, Ms. Svengali," he said, still chuckling. "Exactly how long have you been plotting this one? It's a little humbling to think you've been mapping out your escape route while you were pretending to enjoy my dictation."

He'd meant it to be a compliment, but to his surprise, Ginger's eyes suddenly glistened, though her smile remained intact. "Never fear," she said, and her voice seemed huskier, more vulnerable than he'd ever heard it. "Your dictation has always had my undivided attention." Drew stood up, preparing to cross over to her, but she held up her pink-tipped fingers, stopping him.

"It's just been on my mind since yesterday," she said, blinking the dewy glisten away and deepening her smile. "Ever since I saw that cab in the driveway. A little alarm went off in my mind, you know? It sounded kind of like 'ding-dong, true love calling.'"

What could he say? He'd always known Ginger was much more canny, much more street smart and savvy, than her spun-sugar manner let on. But he hadn't realized how supremely intuitive she really was until this very moment.

He thought of denying her implications, but then he just shook his head. "I don't know, Ginger," he said, deciding to give her the ultimate respect of real, unadulterated honesty. "It could be more like 'bad news calling.' It didn't work out for Laura and me before, you know, and nothing has really changed."

"Hmm." She frowned, obviously surprised to hear that Drew hadn't secured the new bird before letting the old one fly free. "What if it doesn't work out? Have you thought of that, Drew? If you've decided that nothing less than true love will do—well, that can be pretty lonely sometimes. What if old sad eyes stays just long enough to get whatever it is she wants, and then she takes her act back to Boston?"

Drew laughed, but the sound was mirthless. "Believe me, that's the most likely scenario. In fact, she's announced up front that she intends to do just that." Sighing, he ran his hand over his cheek, feeling the scratchy stubble that reminded him he hadn't shaved this morning.

"To tell you the truth, Ginger, I don't really know what happens then. Do you think I'd make a good priest? Or a monk, maybe? That sounds nice and Gothic. Kind of fits the house, don't you think?"

She came to him then and put her hand on his cheek, though the gesture was oddly devoid of flirtation. "The Mad Monk of Winterwalk," she said with a half smile. "I think I like it."

5

IT WAS MIDNIGHT. Outside, the full moon trained a harsh white spotlight on the mounded drifts of snow. The still trees might have been painted onto the landscape.

Inside the tower, an equally hollow silence had reigned for the past hour, and it was driving Drew crazy. Laura's breathing was so slow and soft that, even when he stood in the doorway to her bedroom, he practically had to hold his own breath in order to hear her. The sound both mystified and frustrated him. How could she, who claimed to be grappling with demons in the night, be sleeping so quietly, like a dreamless baby, while he . . . Well, right now he felt as if he might never sleep again.

He was so tired even his bones hurt, but somehow his body felt like a machine permanently set on alert. For no good reason, his heart pumped firmly and rapidly, his shoulders were slightly tensed, and his legs were restless. He'd probably paced off ten miles back and forth across the room in the past hour.

But always, just beyond the flimsy barrier of his self-control, the memories were waiting. Memories of last night, of Laura in his arms, in his bed. It was getting harder and harder to keep them from taking over. Determined, he had for the first few minutes silently recited everything he could remember from the Gallic Wars, the most difficult passages he had been forced to memorize in high-school Latin. But the meager bits he could dredge up after all these years didn't take him far.

Veni, vedi, vici. I came, I saw, I conquered. But even that reminded him of his tragic, false sense of triumph last night, when he had, for one blood-stirring moment, thought he had conquered Laura's fears.

No.

Think of something else. Something productive. Surely he wasn't so spineless that he could only sit here in the eerie moonlight and wait for something to happen. Surely he could think of something to do.

Damian. Perhaps, he thought, pacing again, he should make another stab at tracking down Damian, at forcing the man to come back and face Laura's questions. Yes, that was a good idea.

But was it possible? Though Laura didn't know it, Drew had tried to find her father once before, about four years ago. Drew had been desperate, some sixth sense telling him that time was running out. He had hoped against hope that Damian might know of a childhood trauma that could account for Laura's fears. Drew hadn't suspected that Damian himself might be responsible, but he had wondered whether maybe there'd been an uncle, a gardener, a visiting artist— anyone who might have brought sexual sickness into the Nolan household, into little Laura's life.

Elizabeth Nolan had been no help at all. Drew had always been uneasy around the older woman, and he'd been cravenly reluctant to discuss Laura's problem with her. When he finally approached her about it, she had put him in his place with one withering sentence. "Laura is a lady, Drew, and if you've tried to treat her like a harlot, you've only yourself to blame."

It was then that he had initiated the search for Damian, hiring a private detective to comb the world for a sculptor who might have taken on a new identity in mid-life. Pitiful as it was, it was Drew's only lead, for Damian had had no family left, no one to whom he might have returned when he left Winterwalk.

At any rate, the detective had found nothing. Drew, who had already come into his inheritance, had shelled out thousands, even extending the search to other countries, but always the report had been the same. No one meeting Damian Nolan's description could be found.

Still, he could try one more time.

Suddenly the silence around him was alive with soft rustlings, and he held his breath in earnest, listening. His heart thudded, confusing the sounds even as he strained to distinguish them. Sliding whispers that might have been either sheets or sibilant voices. Was she awake? Was she talking in her sleep? Tossing fitfully? Weeping? Was she frightened? His muscles tensed reflexively, ready to rush to the rescue.

But then, without warning, he saw her, a milky statue in the doorway, touching the cool stone wall beside her with long, pale fingers. Something tortured brushed past Drew's lips at the sight of her. Laura . . . Her hair was streaming down her back, unbound. By lamplight, he remembered from their strained, overformal good-nights, her floor-length nightgown had been blue. But the moonlight drained the flowing fabric of any color, so that it appeared as ghostly white as her skin.

Her eyes were open, catching the moonlight in winking flashes, and though he was prepared this time, he was still shocked by how natural her gaze seemed. Had he not known better, he would have sworn she was awake, that she would in a moment smile apologetically and ask him the time, or request a glass of water.

But she didn't. In silence, with movements as smooth and slow as a mechanical doll, she looked around the room. She looked at the barred window. She looked at his cot. And then she looked at him.

Laura . . . He stood stock-still, his heart pumping so violently he could feel it in his fingertips. But her gaze rested only briefly on his face and then, unrecognizing, moved on. Drew swallowed his disappointment like a pill.

After another minute, she advanced slowly into the room, her gait graceful, free of any self-consciousness or tension. To Drew it seemed she almost floated. The sight was so unnerving that he felt an overwhelming urge to wake her, to make this distant, ethereal creature disappear and to bring back his own real Laura, complete with her human flaws. Tears and anger, even trembling rejection, would have been a welcome relief from this unnatural poise. But he stopped himself, remembering his promise. He mustn't interfere—just follow and stand guard.

She was uncannily agile. She turned the doorknob swiftly and within seconds she had crossed to the narrow, winding stairwell. He noticed that she ignored the elevator, which had been installed only a few years before she moved away, as if she had regressed to a much earlier acquaintance with the house. But she seemed to know the stairs intimately. She took them quickly, her bare feet equally noiseless on the aged wood of the upper floors and the cold stone of the lower levels. Her nightgown pooled on the steps behind her, hiding her feet, which contributed to Drew's disconcerting sensation of having stumbled into someone else's dream.

He followed closely, his skin prickling as her somber profile, just a pale oval below him, moved in and out of the moonlight. Her dark hair seemed to melt into the darkness around her—he hadn't ever realized before that it was the exact color of midnight shadows, but now, he knew, it was one more detail he'd never forget.

When she reached the ground floor, it was clear she was going straight to the conservatory, just as she had told him she would. Watching her maneuver around the furniture, Drew was glad he'd never redecorated the main rooms of the house. Clearly she was operating with some kind of memory radar. Even Drew, who had lived here for three whole years, bumped the edge of an occasional table, jostled the carved arm of a chair here and there, but Laura sailed past it all, her unseeing eyes looking straight ahead, never bothering to check her path.

It wasn't until she reached the conservatory door that she showed any signs of uncertainty. Drew, expecting her to rush in, was caught unaware, and had to stop so close behind her that he could have identified the scent of the sachet in which she'd packed her clothes. He was also near enough to see that the fingers she wrapped around the doorknob were trembling.

She kept her hand there for several long seconds, which were ticked heavily away by the grandfather clock in the hall behind them. Drew moved to the side, where he could see her face. Though her expression was blank, there was a strange helplessness in her posture, in the way she clung to the doorknob, not quite able to turn it. She was as diffident as a child sent on a too-difficult errand, unsure of the way forward but afraid to go back.

Childlike. Drew shook his head, realizing that in some inexplicable way Laura actually had become a child again. But how unlike the children he was familiar with. His sister's daughters were bold and rambunctious and would have noisily barged ahead anywhere, any time, demanding whatever help or attention they needed. Drew's heart pinched, suddenly sure that Laura had never known such boisterous confidence, that as a child she probably had often been paralyzed with insecurity. And fear.

Abruptly, as if propelled by a desperate blast of sheer will, Laura twisted the knob and, flinging the door open, entered the conservatory. She seemed to be past hesitation, past fear. She went straight toward the heart of the huge room, where all the sculptures were clustered. Drew followed her quickly, closing the door behind them.

He stopped two paces in. How exotic everything looked, how transformed by the moonlight, which poured in through thousands of clear glass panes. Because Drew rarely came here at night, he had been subconsciously expecting to enter a warm green world, and he was momentarily stunned by the odd, almost metallic glow around him. The moonlight had painted the plants in subtle shades of silver, white and gray. The entire room shimmered as Laura moved through it, touching a pearled leaf with a fingertip, brushing an argent branch with the long sleeve of her nightgown.

Drew, who was not given to fancies, suddenly had a vision of Laura as one of Damian's statues, miraculously brought to life by this strange silver glow. Graceful, white, stirringly sensual, though only half-real. He watched her intently from the shadows, as if, should he even for an instant take his eyes from her, she might revert to inanimate marble and be lost to him forever.

She passed the mermaid and the dark, glassy pond without giving them a glance. She didn't stop until she reached the marble carving of her own head that stared at her from the breast-high pedestal. It was a curious sight and somehow unsettling—the adult Laura coming face to face with the knowing marble eyes of the child Laura. Rigid from an illogical impulse to stop her, Drew steadied himself against the cool bark of the nearest trunk and took a deep breath. Settle down, he instructed himself. What harm could looking at it do? It was, after all, just a chunk of marble.

He watched as Laura reached out and touched the stone face gently, tilting her head to one side, as if asking the mute child a question. She traced the white curve of the little girl's cheek with two fingers, then stroked her hair, cupping the palm of her hand around her head, as if she offered warmth and comfort.

Then, to Drew's horror, with no warning whatsoever, Laura began to cry. Her mouth opened in a silent moan, and silver tears gleamed like a lining of mercury along her lower lids. She dragged both hands slowly along the statue's head, clutching even as she pulled away, as though she were being wrenched from the child against her will.

Then, as if she received orders from some voice only she could hear, she shut her eyes, the tears dripping in thick, anguished paths down her cheeks, and she brought her shaking hands to her neck, where she clumsily began to unbutton her nightgown.

Drew froze, the hair on his arms raising in a primitive reaction to something profoundly wrong. He had been sympathetic, of course, when Laura had told him

her story of these midnight walks. But he had not understood, not even begun to reckon, how blood-chilling
the reality of this appalling ritual could be. It was a
harrowingly slow process. One button opened, one
inch of pale, silvered skin exposed at a time. Drew tried
to swallow and, failing, choked slightly, but she didn't
seem to hear him.

She bowed her head, dropping her small, pointed
chin almost to her breastbone, and her fingers continued their dreadful labors.

Finally the gown was fully open, and still silently
weeping, Laura eased it from her shoulders. It fell to the
ground around her feet, just as it had done last night.
But this was different, so shockingly different. Oh,
God . . . Drew dug his fingers into the trunk, flecks of
bark penetrating painfully under his nails. Why had he
promised not to interrupt her ordeal? His legs ached
from the need to go to her, and his heart was pounding, bruising his ribs.

She was too beautiful for this, he thought incoher-
ently, his thoughts strangling on his flooding emotions. Too beautiful to suffer so. Instantly the moon
claimed her, capturing her in its garish searchlight, as
if she had been required to present herself for its cold
inspection. And she allowed it. Like a prisoner, she
submitted to it, though her tears came so fast now that
they traced a shining path down her neck, across her
collarbone, curving down the graceful swell of one
breast.

No, damn it. No! Unable to bear it another minute,
Drew reached out, catching her naked body in his arms
just as the last of her courage seemed to drain away, and
she began to sink to her knees.

"Laura, darling," he murmured, folding her up against his pounding heart. "Oh, God, Laura." He wrapped his arms around her, as if he could, by shielding her from the moonlight, protect her from whatever magnetic evil had drawn her here. "It's all right, sweetheart," he whispered. "It's going to be all right."

But Laura didn't hear him. As soon as his arms touched her, she had gone completely limp. With a long, low sigh she had turned her face into his shoulder, and her whole body had relaxed against him. Like an exhausted, frightened child who has finally endured too much, Laura had retreated into sleep.

THE MINUTE she woke up, Laura knew she had walked in her sleep. She could feel the cool kiss of satin against her naked breast, and her legs slid easily across the slick sheets, unimpeded by her nightgown.

The knowledge didn't startle her at first. It had happened a hundred mornings in her life. But then she raised herself up on one elbow, holding the blanket to her chest, and saw her blue gown draped neatly, carefully, across the foot of the bed

She lay back, scalded. She knew, with a helpless certainty, what the nightgown meant. This morning wasn't like all the others. It wasn't her mother who had tucked her naked, tear-stained body into bed last night. It was Drew.

She groaned, thinking of Drew carrying her upstairs, placing her carefully between the sheets. Drew, who had never seen her naked before. Drew, who had once hungered to be her lover. Drew, who had once adored her, thought her worthy of taking his name, bearing his children, sharing his life. With a low cry, she turned her head into the pillow, a sharp pain digging into her throat as she fought stupid tears. He would never feel those things for her again. How could he, after this?

In a way, it shocked her to discover how much she hated the thought of him seeing her like that. She had assured herself he was the perfect person to turn to because he'd always known she was troubled, mixed-up, hung up. Whatever euphemism she chose, he'd long since come to grips with it.

But this was different, infinitely worse. Now he knew she was really, truly crazy.

She lay there a long time, staring at the rounded tower walls, before she felt ready even to stand up. To her relief, when she did finally climb out of bed, pulling the gown tightly around herself, Drew was gone. Perhaps he'd guessed she'd need time to compose herself before she faced him again.

She spent an obsessive hour dressing, finally picking from her limited wardrobe a pair of black stirrup pants and an oversize delft blue sweater, in which she felt comfortably asexual. Her body seemed foreign to her this morning, she thought, checking all angles in the bathroom mirror, making sure her curves were thoroughly hidden. It was strangely as if her body now belonged more to him than to herself. Quelling a deep shiver at the thought of him looking at her, learning at his leisure all the intimate secrets he must have thought he'd never know, she pulled her hair into a tight ponytail and decided to forgo makeup. Of all things, she didn't want to look as if she was trying to be sexy. What, she wondered, could be less sexy than a crazy lady who wandered around, confused and naked and out of control?

She found him in his office, two floors down. Ginger was with him, her classy beige and white business suit hugging all the right places, proclaiming her professionalism and her sexuality in one crisply tailored statement. Watching the secretary bend over Drew's shoulder, reading the document he was holding, Laura had to fight down a spurt of spiteful jealousy. In that moment, she would have given three small kingdoms to be able to trade places with Ginger. Or, as a second choice, to be able to beam the blonde right off the planet.

Drew and Ginger both looked up as Laura entered, and Laura wondered whether that odd expression in Drew's eye was embarrassment. And didn't Ginger's stare have perhaps an extra measure of avid speculation? But when Laura looked closer, both of them seemed perfectly normal, perhaps just a little curious as to why she had interrupted them. She shook herself mentally. She couldn't go around reading significance into every lift of Drew's brow, every minute alteration of the set of his lips. And surely, surely he wouldn't ever have spoken of this to Ginger.

Well, whether he had or not, this definitely wasn't the moment to ask him exactly what had happened last night. Fighting the urge to cross her arms protectively over her breasts, she raised her chin and straightened her shoulders.

"I just wanted to tell you I'm going out for a walk," she lied, and then she felt her face flame violently as she realized that the word "walk" had taken on embarrassing implications. God, what next? "Sex" and "love" had been verboten for years. If she didn't get hold of herself, she'd be reduced to communicating in grunts.

Drew dropped the document on his desk casually, seemingly unaware of her confusion. "Better not go far. They're predicting snow this afternoon."

Rationally, Laura knew it was merely a friendly warning, but the miserable demon in her chose to take offense. Don't go far? Did he now consider her so helpless and incompetent that she needed a leash, a keeper? Don't let the crazy lady wander far. No telling what she'll do to embarrass us in front of the neighbors.

"Don't worry about me," she replied stiffly. "I can take care of myself."

Instantly, even before he raised his brows quizzically, she was ashamed.

There was no need to snipe at him. He was just being polite, a careful host. She, on the other hand, was being a jerk, letting her acute sense of humiliation overrule her manners. Maybe he had even been hinting that he wouldn't be long with Ginger, that soon they would be able to talk privately.

"Well, at least in broad daylight I can," she amended with a small smile, hoping he understood it was an apology. With Ginger curiously looking from one to the other of them, she couldn't say anything more explicit.

"Fine, then," Drew said, picking up his document again. Laura understood that she was being dismissed. "Have fun."

WHEN the first flakes began to fall, Laura had been walking for about an hour, long enough to work up a pleasant burn in her legs, long enough to visit most of her favorite places on the estate. She had always liked the grounds of Winterwalk better than the house. They were spacious and beautifully landscaped and normal.

Or nearly normal. There was, after all, the issue of the boat landing. In keeping with the Venetian flavor of the house, the architect had decided to put an authentic Italian dock out on the eastern edge of the grounds. It didn't matter that Winterwalk was miles from the nearest body of water. The ornate dock floated here under the trees, just as if someone might need to tether his gondola to one of its brilliantly glazed terracotta pillars.

Laura had always loved the wide, open platform of the dock, and the silly birds and fish that had been carved into the trim. She had spent many hours here, dreaming, and Drew had often asked her why she appreciated the nonsense of a landlocked dock when she couldn't understand the whimsy of Winterwalk itself. She hadn't been able to answer him very well, except to say that she could breathe better out here.

It was there Drew found her, staring at the white sea of snow that rolled out in all directions.

"Still waiting for your ship to come in?"

It was an old joke. "Waiting for my captain to come home," she would have answered once, long ago, turning happily into his arms, meeting his kiss.

Today, though the words sprang to her lips as naturally as bubbles from a spring, she forced them back, unspoken.

"Hello, Drew," she said, wincing at the formality of it, but unable to do better. She felt tongue-tied from the effort to avoid saying the wrong things, the old things.

"Hi." Drew smiled at her, and she found herself smiling back. He looked different somehow. She studied his face for a second, and then all at once she realized the change was merely in his clothes. He had abandoned his suit for a thick, cream-colored turtleneck sweater, brown suede jacket and casual brown pants. He looked wonderful, the perfect country gentleman. Two pairs of ice skates were slung over his shoulder, one black, one white.

"Where's Ginger?" she inquired politely, ignoring the skates. "Work all done?"

"All done," he echoed. "We bought everything there was to buy, sold everything there was to sell, so we decided to call it a day."

"Wow. And it's not even noon yet." She couldn't quite figure out what to make of his lighthearted tone. He sounded a little like someone visiting a sick relative, determined to buoy her spirits, to take her mind off her illness. "Now what?"

"And now," he answered with mock solemnity, "you and I, madam, are going to take my nieces and nephews ice-skating on the pond."

She laughed, incredulous. "I am? I don't even have any skates!"

He dropped one shoulder, sliding the white skates free with a flourish. "Your skates, my lady."

Unbelievably, they *were* her skates. She had left them behind when she'd left. They must have been somewhere among all that clutter in the attic. How amazing that he'd been able to find them! She touched the flashing blade with her fingertip. It was as cold and sharp as an icicle.

Every winter since they were children, she and Drew had skated together on the pond between their two estates. Once, when they had rushed the season a bit, the too thin ice had cracked beneath her, and Drew had had to pull her out. The memory saddened her somehow. Poor Drew. He had practically made a career out of rescuing her, hadn't he?

"I don't have the right kind of socks," she demurred, reluctant to relive those memories. Sometimes the gentle memories seemed even harder to face than the frightening ones. They could do more than make you walk in your sleep. They could break your heart.

He dug in the pocket of his jacket. "Socks," he said smugly, dangling a pair of thick, diamond-patterned woolen socks in front of her. He rooted around some more. "And gloves. And a hat."

She laughed, letting him fill her arms with it all. "Good heavens. Anything else in there?"

He patted his pockets, double-checking. "I'm not sure. I may have the baby grand in here somewhere, too."

Their smiling gazes locked, and Drew put out his hand. Laura felt herself succumbing. Why not, she thought, suddenly ready to defy the grim gods who seemed so determined to tie her life in knots. They were the gods of the night. They had no power over days like this, days that were a frosty, windswept blue, days when Drew stood next to her, holding out his hand, inviting her to forget for a little while.

Why not? She knew all too well the answer to that self-indulgent question. But, ignoring it, she took his hand and stepped off the dock into the river of snow.

IT WAS a glorious afternoon—perhaps the most wonderful afternoon she had ever spent, she thought with an expansive, swelling happiness as she looped the pond one more time, little Nina's hand in hers. Stephanie's children were enchanting, though certainly not angels, she admitted, feeling the most recent snowball melting along her hairline. They were far too normal to be angels. But they were lovely and loving, high-

spirited and clever. And, because they adored their
uncle Drew, they embraced Uncle Drew's lady friend,
as well.

Laura had met them all, though they didn't remember her. The older ones, fair-haired boys who looked
disarmingly like Drew, were now seven and six years
old, cocky second and first graders, but they'd been just
toddlers when Laura left Winterwalk. And the two little girls, Cindy and Nina, were only four and five, respectively, and thus they hadn't been much more than
infants when Laura last saw their mother.

Suddenly Nina tripped, clutching at Laura's hand for
support. "Whoa," Laura said, balancing herself as she
tugged the little girl into a fully upright position.
"Careful!"

Nina smiled at her, her tiny features miraculously,
perfectly Townsend already. Especially her smile.
Laura's heart thumped once, hard. Is this what it would
have been like to have Drew's daughter? "I'm not very
good yet," Nina confided, as if Laura couldn't possibly
have guessed it on her own. "Mommy says I'm getting
better every day, but Brett says I stink."

Brett, who at that moment was barreling by them as
if he was in an Olympic competition, *would* have said
that, Laura thought. He was a born athlete and clearly
already a gold medalist in his mind. But, though both
boys teased their sisters mercilessly, Laura had watched
them helping the girls lace their skates, and she knew
there was a lot of love among them all.

"Cindy stinks even worse than I do," Nina said
proudly, pointing to her little sister, who was stumbling along at Drew's side. "Pee-yew!"

As they watched, Drew seemed to decide the little girl
had struggled enough. He scooped her up and hoisted

her onto his shoulders. Cindy squealed with delight and immediately began issuing orders from her lofty perch. "Faster!" she cried. "Over there. No, go over there. Over *there!*"

Drew skated smoothly, his long legs easily gliding across the ice, obeying his niece's queenly edicts without hesitation. Nina made a small, discontented sound, as if she suddenly realized there might be advantages to being the youngest, even if you did stink. Laura made a small sound herself, though she hoped Nina didn't hear it. It held an unmistakable note of longing. How lucky these children were to belong to Drew, to have a forever claim on his love and attention, not to be, as she was, counting out their time with him in stolen afternoons and midnight madness.

But then, as if he could sense that Laura was feeling odd man out, he deposited Cindy on the bench at the end of the pond and skated over to them.

"Time out, half-pint," he said with a smile. "Go take a break with your sister."

Nina began to whine, but silenced herself immediately when Drew lowered his brows. Dispiritedly but without further comment, she hobbled off toward the bench, her short, choppy steps much less graceful now that she had no adult to cling to.

Laura smiled, acknowledging the deft juggling act he'd been doing all afternoon, how cleverly he'd rotated his attention from one child to the next, giving them each their time to bask in the spotlight of his affection. How like him not to leave her out, either. "My turn, Uncle Drew?"

His answering smile was blinding. "On the contrary." He tucked her hand warmly in his. "It's my turn."

They didn't talk much as, hand in hand, they swept across the pond, their strides matching well. Of course, she reminded herself carefully, his stride had matched Brett's, too, and then Cindy's. It was his gift.

But still, they felt so right together. Gradually the warmth of his hand seeped through the leather of their gloves, and she tightened her grip, seeking it blindly.

Their breath misted in the cold, mingled and then blew across their faces. It was such a beautiful day. A blue light sparkled through the white-limbed trees, which bent protectively over the small round pond. A few airy flakes of new snow drifted around their shoulders. They went all the way around the pond, then began the circle once more. Again, Laura had the sensation of being deep inside her snow globe, twirling safely in a universe of their own. How did he do that, she wondered? How did he manage to create the sensation of being protected, shielded from the rest of the world? He hadn't even said a word.

Suddenly she realized that he had shifted the pattern of their rotation and was steering them toward the empty bench on the far side of the pond, away from where the children were absorbed in some game that involved twigs and snowballs.

One ancient oak, nearly bent double with age, hid the corner of the bench from view, and Drew brought her to a smooth stop right there, behind the snow-laden branches. They sat side by side on the bench, thigh to thigh and shoulder to shoulder, their breath puffing in gentle, rapid clouds as they recovered from their exertions. She hadn't realized how fast they had been skating until now, when the swirling world finally came to a halt, like a merry-go-round whose ride is over.

"Just about time to head home, I think," Drew said, and Laura tried to interpret the tone in his voice. Was he relieved? Disappointed? But he simply sounded factual, and she couldn't honestly read anything further into it.

"Stephanie's getting ready for her birthday party," he added conversationally. "That's why I've got the kids—to keep them out of her hair. She's always crazy the day before a party."

Stephanie's birthday. Laura searched her memory and found the date. Of course it was. "I'd forgotten," she said slowly. "It's amazing, but I'd actually forgotten what day her birthday was."

He didn't seem disturbed by the admission. "Well, she's hoping you'll come to the party," he said. He looked at Laura. "She's eager to see you."

"She is?" Laura couldn't help sounding dubious. Though Stephanie was five years older than Laura, the two women had once been good friends. But that was before Laura broke off her engagement to Drew. She had received only one letter from Stephanie after that, and it had been harsh and unforgiving.

"Very. I told her you were here, and she made me promise to bring you." He frowned, finally seeming to notice her unsettled expression. "That's okay, isn't it? I actually thought you'd be glad. It'll give you and Stephanie time to talk about things. About Damian."

Laura still didn't answer. It would seem so strange to dress up in fancy clothes and go to a party, just as if she was still part of this world. "I don't know," she said doubtfully. "I'm not sure I'm up to it just now...."

"Nonsense." Drew seemed impatient. "You want to get to the bottom of all this, don't you?"

"Of course."

"Then you need to talk to Stephanie. We don't have to stay all night if you don't want to." He reached over and patted her hand, just as if she was another sister. "You'll do fine."

"All right," she said reluctantly, looking at his strong hand over hers. "I guess it'll be all right."

He took her capitulation in stride. Releasing her hand, he looked at the children, still on the bench, still absorbed in their strange game.

"We really had better go," he said again, but he made no move to get up.

"The kids will be tired," she agreed, trying to match the impersonal quality he seemed to find so easily. "This is a lot of exercise."

"Especially for the little ones," he added. Laura felt a sense of keen frustration. Here they were, alone together in this haven created by the snow and the oaks and the pond, and they were saying nothing more meaningful than the idle chitchat they might have offered a stranger.

She wanted more. She wanted to connect. But she laced her gloved fingers together in her lap and stared at them, unable to think of anything to say.

"I'm a little tired myself," he said, and running his hands through his hair, he yawned broadly.

Of course he was. Laura squeezed her fingers together so hard they hurt. Of course he was tired—he'd been up all night, following her through the house, trying to make sure she didn't do anything stupid, anything dangerous. And she hadn't even thanked him for it.

"I'm sorry," she said quietly. "That's my fault, I know."

"God, Laura, it's not anyone's fault," he said quickly, turning toward her.

Laura's gaze dropped, her cheeks burning against the cold snowflakes.

"Hey." Drew nudged her with his elbow. "It's okay, Laura. Really, it's okay."

She shook her head, not contradicting him, exactly, but not quite believing.

"I haven't thanked you," she said awkwardly, unable to continue the charade of holiday high spirits. She wasn't here for a holiday—how could she have allowed herself to forget that? "For last night. I know it can't have been pleasant."

To her relief, he didn't pretend to misunderstand her. "No need to thank me," he said in low tones. "I was glad I could help."

She could feel his gaze on her, serious now, but she couldn't look at him. Instead she looked out across the grounds where, just beyond the farthest treetops, the chimneys of Springfields could be glimpsed. What must he, who had grown up around such easy normalcy, such ordered restraint, think of the macabre chaos of her life now?

Suddenly she felt strangely frantic for him to tell her about it, as if she couldn't stand to go on without knowing what it had been like. Exactly. With all the details her mother had never been willing to tell her.

"Drew," she said, compelled to pursue it, though she suspected, from his manner today, that he'd rather not. Just like her mother, really, who had always tacitly communicated that Laura's aberrant behavior ought never to be mentioned in the morning. She had pulled a veil of silence over it, the way she might have hung a picture over a stain on the wall, preserving the illusion

that everything was fine. But somehow the pretense had
only made Laura feel worse, giving her imagination full
scope to invent horrors for herself. If her actions were
so disgusting they couldn't be discussed in polite soci-
ety, she had deduced, then they must be terrible indeed.

"Drew, was it awful?" She hardly knew how to ask
it, but she had to. That was what she was here for, after all. "Do I look . . . Do I act . . ." She turned to him,
her inner turmoil rising sharply, dangerously. She felt
almost as if she was choking. "Is it just too horrible, as
if I'm a madwoman? When I'm naked . . . is it . . . vulgar?"

For a long moment Drew stared at her, silent. His eyes
narrowed against a quick flurry of snowflakes, and it
gave his face a look of sudden intensity, almost of anger. Then he took her hand and held it fast in his. He
gripped her so hard she could feel the strong bones of
his fingers even through the leather.

"It's very sad," he said finally, his voice low and
husky, vibrating with an unsettling emotion. "And it's
very beautiful."

He frowned, and his face tightened, as if he was in
pain. "I think," he said, "that you're perhaps the most
breathtaking, heartbreaking woman I've ever seen."

6

THE NEXT DAY, Laura almost changed her mind a dozen times about going to Stephanie's birthday party. When, sometime around eight o'clock, she found herself actually in the car, driving toward Springfields, she hardly knew how she had ended up there. She'd meant to tell Drew she had a headache, a fever, a dizzy spell—anything—but he'd spent most of the day in town, and somehow she just hadn't found the right time or the right words to do it.

Now here she was, pulling up the drive, dressed in a slinky silver gown she'd found in the attic, and it was too late to back out. Springfields lay before her, and she caught her breath, as entranced as ever. The neoclassical mansion rose out of the crest of a snowy hill, its Doric columns white and resplendent—an ice temple fired by torches and starlight.

She glanced at Drew, suddenly attacked anew by insecurity. Why had he invited her? She didn't belong here anymore, didn't have any right to let her emotional darkness cast a shadow on all this gleaming perfection.

"Drew..." she began hesitantly.

"There's probably going to be a big crowd," Drew said, as if she had asked him a question. Perhaps she had, with her nervous glance and restive hands, which she kept twisting in her lap. He knew her well enough to interpret those clues correctly. "Huge. You know how Stephanie is."

Laura nodded. Stephanie loved people—all kinds, all ages—and had an intense, sympathetic curiosity about them. "Oh, he's had *such* an interesting life," she'd say about anyone she met, from a U.S. senator to the kid who delivered her groceries. It always took her hours to complete even the simplest errands, because she'd "get talking," as she apologetically put it, and lose track of time. But she'd come home knowing absolutely everything about the postman who weighed her package, the cashier who rang up her new purse, the stylist who cut her hair.

"Drew," Laura began again, but they had pulled up to the front entrance, and Drew was still talking amiably, whisking off his seat belt. She didn't touch hers.

"The Milfords will be there, and the Brightons—" He stopped as the uniformed valets, well choreographed, opened both doors at once, and suddenly there was nothing for Laura to do but climb out as gracefully as possible. Drew handed the keys to the valet and quickly joined Laura at the foot of the steps.

The Milfords and the Brightons. Laura looked up the tall flight of stairs, wondering how she'd find the courage to do this. Once she had believed that Springfields would be her home, that she and Drew would live here and raise their family in this, the Townsend family estate. She had expected to be the one hosting parties here, standing next to her handsome, adoring husband and greeting silly Mildred Milford and quiet Dolly Brighton and all the rest of the well-bred, well-to-do people she'd grown up with.

Three years ago she'd given up that dream, and now the names came to her with a queer sense of sadness, as if someone was reading her a list of the dead. But they weren't dead. She could hear them now, laughing and murmuring and clinking ice in their favorite cocktails. She could see, through the wide, undraped windows, the shadows of their faces, the sparkle of their diamonds, the swirling dabs of color as their beautiful dresses danced by. They were very much alive, going on with their lives the way they always had.

Actually, she thought as she numbly let Drew lead her up the stairs, it would be more accurate to say that *she* was the one who had died. The Laura Nolan they knew was gone. In her place was this obsessively normal young woman, who lived in a neat little Boston town house that looked just like everyone else's, who worked day after day as the recreation coordinator for a chain of nursing homes just as if she needed the money. She wondered if they would even recognize her.

"Laura!" A soft cry broke into her thoughts, and Laura suddenly felt herself enveloped in Stephanie's eager embrace. "Laura, it's so good to see you!" Stephanie drew back to study her face. "Oh, kiddo, you look wonderful!"

Overwhelmed, Laura simply shook her head and smiled, relieved. Other hurdles might still lie ahead, but the most important question was answered. Apparently Stephanie had decided to forgive Laura for running away from her beloved brother. Perhaps, Laura thought suddenly, wondering why it had never occurred to her before, perhaps Stephanie had finally realized that Laura had done Drew a favor by setting him free.

Still, she was glad Drew hadn't taken his hand away from her elbow. It was a steady warmth, reassuring and strong.

"You look pretty marvelous yourself," Laura said, returning the hug. It was true. Stephanie was immensely pregnant, but radiant in a honey silk ball gown that was exactly the same color as her hair. Laura had almost forgotten how much lighter Stephanie's hair was than Drew's.

"Hey, everyone—Laura's here!" Stephanie called in her inimitable, breezy style, as if the whole party had been waiting for her arrival. And suddenly Laura was in the center of a small storm of welcoming faces— Stephanie's husband, Mark, all the children, the children's nanny, and then dozens of guests, from Mildred Milford and Dolly Brighton, with husbands in tow, to people Laura hadn't thought about in three years. Everyone professed to be thrilled to see her, and most of them even sounded sincere. If, among the faces, there were one or two who seemed sharp with curiosity, Laura didn't have time to dwell on it. There were too many hands to shake, kisses to accept, questions to ask and answer.

She couldn't have done it without Drew. At first it was just the security of his presence that kept her going. Then, as the more casual acquaintances came up for their turns, he jogged her memory with a perfectly placed sentence. "Oh, Mrs. Blankenship, come tell Laura about Betty's scholarship to Harvard. Back when she used to baby-sit for you she'd always tell me how smart Betty was!" And Mrs. Blankenship would never realize that Laura had nearly forgotten her.

Soon, though, Laura was making the connections herself. It was as if, now that she had relaxed a bit, her memories could flow freely. The librarian, the school principal, the widow from the estate on the far side of

Springfields—they all paraded before her, sweeping her back into their world as if she'd never been gone.

Very strange, she thought, listening to Reverend Mosier complain about the rotted wood in the steeple—the same crisis he'd been collecting money for three years ago. Had so little changed, then? She'd felt as if she'd been gone a lifetime, but obviously to everyone else it had been only three short, rather uneventful years. No one thought much of her absence, really. She'd been gone longer than this when she went off to college.

Suddenly Laura felt a rush of affection for them all, for the way they had innocently held a place for her, perhaps believing she'd be back. In their minds, it seemed, this was her world, no matter how far away she ran. How very sweet. How very strange.

She turned to say something about it to Drew, but to her surprise he was no longer at her side. Her spirits sank suddenly. When did he leave? Was it during Mildred's long-winded litany of the travails of being married to a doctor, or perhaps during Dolly's account of her two-year-old son, who seemed to be a musical prodigy? She checked the room as subtly as she could, hoping not to hurt the reverend's feelings. But Drew was nowhere in sight.

"And you remember your father donated a lovely sculpture for the sanctuary," the reverend was saying, and Laura felt her heart begin to throb swollenly. She plucked at the high neckline of the silver lamé gown, which suddenly felt too tight. Where was Drew?

She scanned the crowd. Where was he? She felt a little like the elephant who had been given a magic feather that could enable him to fly. As long as he held the feather, he stayed safely afloat. But when he dropped it . . .

Finally she found him. He was across the room, talking to a laughing Mildred Milford. Looking up, he caught her eye and, making the thumbs-up sign, tossed her a quick wink before he returned his attention to Mildred.

It was enough. She braced herself with a deep breath, and somehow she got through the reverend's discussion of Damian's sculpture. She could do this. When the minister moved on to chat with other members of his flock, Laura found herself circulating almost comfortably, greeting old acquaintances, hearing the newest gossip until she felt almost at home again, almost as if she had never left. She always knew where Drew was and who he was talking to, but she never again felt the childish need for him to come back and prop her up.

Eventually, though, she tired—her nights hadn't been particularly restful lately. Somehow, without offending anyone, she hoped, she found her way to the back porch, a long, glassed-in room that overlooked the family gardens. It was colder out here, and she leaned against the glass, letting its hard, frigid strength seep into her where the gown's split back bared her skin, and took deep, conscious breaths of the chilled air.

She shouldn't stay long. But she'd give herself one more minute and appreciate the serenity of the snow-quiet garden. She would draw peace from it.

It was a very cold, clear night, and the garden was enchanting, all silver blue snow that glittered with starlight. The focal point of the landscaping was a rectangular pond with a marble fountain carved by Damian. It was emptied now, winterized, and the fountain had been sensibly shut off. But Laura had seen the fountain in its summer glory, shooting rainbowed sprays around the central figure of a young girl whose lovely face was upturned to feel the droplets dancing on her cheeks, whose hands were outstretched to revel in the cool, wet kiss of the water.

It was one of Damian's best works—Stephanie at about fourteen, if Laura remembered correctly. Odd, she thought, that the statue had always seemed utterly innocent, in spite of the way the girl's soaked dress clung to her pubescent body, outlining her small breasts and boyish thighs as clearly as if she'd been naked. But it had never seemed lecherous or erotic. It was simply a lovely work of art, a celebration of the health and gaiety of youth.

Laura stared at the girl, whose outstretched palms were filled with snow, and still saw nothing lewd. Was it possible, she asked herself, that this statue really was different from all the others? Or did it just seem so because it was here at Springfields? Perhaps all the marble children might have seemed equally chaste if they'd been displayed here. Perhaps it was only at Winterwalk that everything seemed contaminated. If so, Laura thought, closing her eyes, she should stand here forever, drinking the pure air of this garden.

But suddenly, as though he had been looking for her, Drew was there, draping her silver-flecked black shawl around her shoulders, covering her bare back. "Tired?" he asked softly, letting his hands rest where her neck and shoulders met.

She shook her head, accepting his appearance quietly, as if they had planned this assignation. She was glad he was here. Though her floor-length gown had long, tight sleeves and a high neck, the slit in the back had let the cold air slip in to caress her skin, and she suddenly realized she was shivering. The heat of his hands sent delicious waves of warmth down from her collarbone, across her chest and over her stomach.

"No, not tired," she said, her voice equally soft, as if they were sharing important secrets rather than pleasantries. "I was just thinking."

"About what?"

"About this house. It occurred to me that if Winterwalk had been more like Springfields, more serene and simple, my life might have been very different."

Drew chuckled, a low, mellow sound that drifted on the clear air. "Not a gargoyle in sight," he agreed, and in spite of his surface amusement, she knew that he understood.

"That's right." She sighed, leaning back just a little, as if her body instinctively sought the warmth of his. "Thumper and Fifi and Bucko scared me to death. They still do."

He chuckled again, and they stood in companionable silence for a long moment. She knew they were both remembering. There were good things to remember, too, weren't there?

"Actually, though, you may have a point." He rubbed her shoulders absently, as if it helped him to think better. "I can see that Winterwalk might have held a nightmarish quality for a young, impressionable girl."

Laura nodded, as tranquil for the moment as if that impressionable girl had been someone else. "All those shadowy, twisting stairs." She smiled at the symmetrical garden, so invulnerable here in Drew's arms that she could afford to pity that young, frightened Laura. "All those stalactite carvings in the ceiling over my bed..."

"Yes. Definitely the stuff of nightmares. And, frankly, it might also have been easier for you," he went on, his tone musing, "if your mother had been more—well, more simple, too."

She stiffened. "In what way?"

She knew in what way. She knew even before he began to verbalize it. But she had always defended her mother, who had had no one else to defend her. It was a hard habit to break.

"I don't know, exactly. More relaxed, I guess." He seemed to be searching for nonjudgmental phrases. "More easygoing. With more of a sense of humor. Your mother took everything hard, didn't she? Made heavy weather out of everything. Remember the time she caught us in the rose garden?"

Of course she remembered. Laura had been only eighteen, and her mother had been rabid with fury, vicious in her condemnation of the pair of would-be lovers. As humiliated as Laura was to be caught lying in the grass at midnight, Drew half on top of her, she had been even more ashamed for Drew to witness one of her mother's rages. And the worst of it was, they hadn't really been doing anything. They never really did anything, did they? But her mother hadn't believed a word of it. Drew had been sent home, and Laura had been forced to stay up all night, first under her mother's hysterical interrogation and then left alone in the dark, vaulted front hall, in the most uncomfortable antique chair, to contemplate her sins.

"She was just trying to protect me," Laura said, struggling to keep any disloyalty out of her voice. Elizabeth's reactions had often been excessive, but she had loved her adopted daughter fiercely. "If Damian had been there, it would have been his job to box your ears and send you packing. But she was alone. She had to be both mother and father to me. So if occasionally she went a little overboard, I think it was understandable."

Drew dropped his hands, a low growl of frustration replacing the earlier chuckle. "You always defend her, Laura. But you know as well as I do that she wasn't like other people. All those years after Damian left, when she practically didn't get out of bed—"

"She was frail," Laura interrupted heatedly, though she knew she was only falling into the old patterns, the old arguments. "She was very fragile . . ."

Drew grabbed her shoulders, his eyes glittering sharply, reflecting the silver gleam of her dress. "Fragile? Damn it, Laura, face it! She was—" He broke off, as if he suddenly realized that what he'd been going to say was unacceptable. He lowered his voice. "She was emotionally unstable. Maybe Damian did that to her and maybe not. I don't know. All I know is that her ranting about how anything sexual was dirty and debasing was enough to upset any girl your age. All that blather about how you were a lady and ladies didn't, shouldn't, couldn't!" His hands tightened, as if he wanted to shake her, but somehow he stopped himself and kept his voice under control. "For God's sake, Laura, it's no wonder you grew up...ambivalent about sex. You don't have to blame Damian for that. You don't have to look any further than the frigid woman who adopted you!"

As he spoke, Laura's blood had, in one sickening swoop, rushed to her hands and feet, and she felt suddenly cold and dizzy. How could he say such things? He'd always been less sympathetic toward her mother than she was, but never had he voiced such harsh, unforgiving sentiments. Laura found it terribly unsettling, as if she suddenly saw her mother through Drew's eyes. It was a strangely frightening sight. Was it possible that he was right? Had her mother's extreme aversion to any hint of her daughter's sexuality warped Laura, too?

No. Laura's emotional clarity returned with a flash of certainty, the way a sudden streak of lightning can illuminate a dark landscape. No, it wasn't possible. It wasn't possible because it simply wasn't enough. There had to be more.

"You're wrong, Drew," she said. "I'm not ambivalent about sex. I'm *terrified*."

She pulled out of his clutches, touching the window for support, and stared unseeing into the garden.

"Have you really forgotten what it was like, Drew? Have you forgotten that I couldn't breathe, that I choked and coughed and sputtered as if I was dying?" She bit her lower lip, aware of what a disgusting picture of herself she was drawing. But it was the truth. "Do you remember how my muscles used to clench so hard that sweat poured from my whole body? What about the day I fainted?"

She turned to him, trembling. "God, Drew, ambivalent? Can you possibly have forgotten how terrible it was?"

His face looked gray, and she knew that she had finally shaken his composure. "No," he said clearly, though his voice was brittle and his jaw was set so hard it looked chiseled from granite. "I haven't forgotten a single thing that ever happened between us, Laura."

"Then stop blaming my mother," she said, feeling suddenly flat, deflated, as if the whole argument had been idiotic. She might have won this battle, but they had both lost the war. Nothing was accomplished by proving what it wasn't, not if they couldn't prove what it was.

Oh, this really was hopeless, wasn't it? She didn't even know anymore what she was doing here in Albany. Argue as bitterly as they might, shoving blame back and forth like a hockey puck across the ice, phrasing and rephrasing, thinking and rethinking whatever they did, they never seemed to get any closer to the truth.

But then, with another shocking insight, she suddenly saw that learning the truth wasn't the only reason she had come back to Winterwalk. It wasn't even the main reason. The real reason was one she had hidden even from herself. She had come because she'd hoped that her mother's death had somehow broken the invisible bonds that held her prisoner in her own body. She'd hoped that maybe, just maybe, the past had died with Elizabeth Nolan.

Suddenly, the need to find out was overwhelming. She wanted Drew to take her in his arms. Right now. She wanted him to try again, to see if anything had changed. She wanted him to want her.

But he didn't. Holding back the swell of tears, she forced herself to face the fact. He had another woman, a beautiful, sophisticated woman who was easy to love. He had no interest in conducting potentially distressing sexual experiments with Laura for old times' sake. He'd been alone with her time after time—he'd even carried her naked body against his heart—and he hadn't once been moved to so much as kiss her. He had simply treated her with the affectionate concern he might have given his sister, nothing more.

She tried to tell herself she should be grateful for that, but she wasn't. She wanted more. Her heart wouldn't stop aching from wanting more.

Kiss me, Drew. She almost said the words aloud, but then out of the corner of her eye she saw Stephanie open the French doors, apparently having chosen that moment to come looking for them.

"Stephanie," Drew called instantly, as if he was relieved to have someone to whom he could shift his burden, the burden of Laura's neurosis. His voice was still so tight and drawn he sounded like a stranger. Stephanie, who had been trying to ease back into the ballroom without being seen, hesitated. She obviously thought Drew and Laura were having a romantic interlude on the porch and didn't want to interrupt. If only she knew, Laura thought with an inner hysteria. If only she knew.

"Hi, there," Stephanie answered, joining them with as much nonchalance as she could muster. "Getting some fresh air?" She fanned herself with her graceful fingertips. "Good idea. It's an oven in there."

"Stephanie, Laura needs to talk to you," Drew said, ignoring the small talk. He met his sister's questioning gaze bluntly. "She'll tell you what it's about. See if you can help her," he said, putting his hand on Stephanie's shoulder, much as he had done to Laura only moments ago. Turning, he looked at Laura one last time. "God knows I can't."

And then he was gone. Stephanie and Laura followed his retreating back with their eyes, and then, when he had disappeared into the crowded ballroom, Stephanie let out a low whistle. "Wow." She looked at Laura curiously. "This sounds serious."

Laura felt ridiculous, like a child shoved into the middle of the living room and forced to recite to strangers. She wasn't even sure how Stephanie felt about her anymore. For all she knew, Stephanie might not be at all inclined to help Drew's ex-fiancée with anything.

"Serious? Well, it might be," Laura said, stalling for time. This was absurd. She couldn't start discussing this now, in the middle of Stephanie's birthday party. "But maybe we can get together for lunch someday soon to talk about it. I'll be here for another week or so. This can't be convenient for you right now."

"Sure it is." Stephanie hoisted herself onto a cushioned window seat and leaned against the glass, her hands folded comfortably across her swollen stomach. She looked perfectly at ease, as if there weren't two hundred people waiting for her to open a mile-high stack of presents and carve up the three-tiered cake. "I need a break from all that in the worst way! So tell Stephie. What's going on?"

Laura had to smile at the way the other woman could erase the years, making them kids again.

"Oh, Stephie," she said, reverting to the old nickname, as Stephanie had no doubt intended she should. "I don't even know where to begin. I don't know what Drew has told you about why I'm back."

"Darn little," Stephanie said with a grimace. "You know Drew. He never even told us why you left in the first place, much less why you're back."

Laura flushed. "I'm sorry about that, about not writing you when I left. I know you were confused— and probably angry, too."

"I certainly was." To Laura's surprise, she found Stephanie's honesty somehow easier to take than any polite denials might have been. "I was mad as hell for a long time. To tell you the truth, I still am, even if I can't help loving you to pieces anyway. You really made a mess of my little brother's heart, you know."

Laura's flush deepened. "I know." She ran her fingertips along the windowsill, which was cold and rough under her fingers. "But he seems to have recovered fairly well. I've met Ginger."

Stephanie made a rude noise. "That . . . Barbie doll? Don't kid yourself. She's a symptom, not a cure."

Laura didn't answer—her feelings were too complicated to express. Was it wrong for her to have hoped that Ginger was not a true love but a reaction? A rebound? Well, she had hoped it, but she was ashamed of herself for doing so. It was selfish and egotistical and utterly unfair.

"So come on!" Stephanie sounded impatient, and she wriggled, trying to settle her bulk more comfortably on the narrow seat. "Are you going to ask for my help or not?"

"All right. This will probably sound really strange," Laura began, wondering how on earth she was going to put it. "It's about Damian."

Stephanie did a double take. "Damian?" she echoed incredulously. "I thought this had to do with Drew."

Laura folded her arms across her chest, nestling her cold fingers under her arms. Why was she so embarrassed to talk about this? She didn't have to tell the other woman anything more than the barest facts. "With Drew? Not exactly," she said. "At least, I don't know if it does. It may. That's part of what I need to ask you."

"Well, *that's* as clear as mud." But Stephanie looked resigned, rubbing her stomach absently. "So ask away. It can't be this hard to find the words, can it?"

Laura smiled awkwardly. "As a matter of fact, it can." She took a deep breath and looked out at the laughing, drenched young girl who had been carved in Stephanie's likeness. It was easier, somehow, to talk to her about this. "But here goes. I wondered whether, while you were posing for Damian, you ever noticed anything that made you uncomfortable. Whether he ever did anything that wasn't quite right."

Stephanie's rubbing stopped slowly, like a wheel rolling to a halt. When Laura looked at her, Stephanie's eyes were narrowed, her expression serious. "Laura Nolan, are you asking what I *think* you're asking?"

Laura just raised her brows, waiting to see what had leaped first into Stephanie's mind.

"Listen here." Stephanie frowned. "Are you asking me whether your father ever made a *pass* at me?"

"My adopted father," Laura corrected automatically, but that was answer enough. Why else would Laura have felt the need to establish the distance between herself and Damian? Why else would she have wanted to remind Stephanie that Damian had been no true blood relation?

Stephanie's eyes widened. "No," she said. "There was never a hint of any such thing. And frankly, if you tell me he made a pass at any of his other models, I'm not going to believe you."

"Why?" Laura caught her breath, stunned by the woman's vehemence.

"Because he wasn't like that." Stephanie couldn't have sounded more certain. "He wasn't a wacko, for heaven's sake. Surely you know that. You lived in the same house with him for ten years. He was your father."

Adopted father. Laura averted her eyes, drawn again to the fountain statue, to the laughing, happy, healthy little girl.

"Well?" Stubbornly persisting, Stephanie obviously wasn't going to let it go now. Laura almost wished she had never brought the subject up. "Well, you didn't really think he was perverted, did you?" She listened to Laura's silence for a moment, and then all at once her voice grew deadly serious. "You did. That's exactly what you thought. Laura, Laura, for God's sake, why?"

Laura pulled her shawl tightly closed in front, suddenly awash with shivers. She'd been standing out here in the cold for too long.

"It's complicated, Stephanie. I don't really know *anything*. I just wonder. I have some problems—" She decided not to elaborate. It was, ultimately, simply too personal. "I'm trying to find out what might have caused them."

"Problems?" Stephanie said the word slowly, and Laura could almost hear the wheels spinning as she processed the implications. Stephanie, in spite of her giddy manner, had an extremely nimble mind. "And Drew is aware of these problems?"

Laura nodded slowly. The snow sparkled like bits of glass through the tears that hung precariously in her eyes, and she didn't dare try to speak.

"All too well, I take it." Stephanie wasn't asking a question. She clearly had it fully sorted out already. She was quiet another moment, and then she cleared her throat decisively. "Well, kiddo, I'll help you any way I can, you know that. But it seems to me the best thing I can do to help is to warn you you're barking up the wrong tree."

Laura still didn't turn around. Two of the tears had spilled, running warm along her cheeks. She traced an invisible figure eight on the window with her fingertip. "Why?"

"Because Damian was a gentleman, that's why. He was unhappy, maybe, and lonely, maybe, but I guarantee you he wasn't easing his loneliness by seducing little girls. I sat for him off and on for years, you know. Lots of times I even sat there while he sculpted you. Do you remember that?"

Laura nodded again, retracing her finger's path. The figure eight. Circles leading to more circles. Infinity. An endless, winding road to nowhere. "I remember."

"Well, you may have been a naive, foggy-minded little kid, but I wasn't." Stephanie lumbered down off the window seat with a pretty groan and smoothed her dress over her stomach. "I was, what, about fifteen? I had sort of discovered boys myself by then, as I recall, so I was particularly tuned in to things like that. If there had been any sexual vibes floating around that room, I would have known it."

She reached out and stopped Laura's nervously tracing finger. "But there weren't. I mean it, Laura. Let it go. It just didn't happen."

7

THE FOLLOWING AFTERNOON, as he sat in the office of Spencer Wilkes, psychiatrist, Drew was already beginning to wonder whether his decision to come had been a wise one.

Drew had just reached the end of his story, and Spencer, who was eating lunch at his big oak desk, froze midbite, his mouth open, his corned beef sandwich poised between his teeth.

He lowered the sandwich. "Good God, Drew," he said slowly.

Drew shifted, hitching his pants leg over his knee with an impatient flick of his fingers. "Spencer," he said, frowning. "If I were one of your paying patients, would you be sitting there gawking and saying 'Good God, Drew'?"

Spencer, who had been one of Drew's best friends and his weekly racquetball partner for several years— but never before his psychiatrist—smiled sheepishly.

"Probably not. But you're not a patient. You're a friend. And when you began this story, the last thing in the world I expected you to say was, 'It turns out she was asleep the whole time.'" He bit into his sandwich, shaking his head. "That's one hell of a punch line."

"It's not a punch line." Drew held back the urge to curse. "This is not a joke."

"I know, I know." The other man wiped his mouth with a paper napkin, then crumpled the napkin into a small ball, tossed it on top of the sandwich and shoved the whole thing to the edge of his desk. "Sorry. I'm not being very professional here, am I? Let's start over."

"Maybe I should have gone to someone else," Drew said, rubbing his temples, which were aching miserably. "Someone I don't know. I can't imagine why I thought this would be easier."

Spencer raised his brows. "To tell you the truth, you probably should have. As your friend, I may be too close to be objective. But as long as you're here, as long as you've already told the sad story once, let's see what I can do." He picked up a pen and scribbled a couple of notes on a blank pad.

Watching him, Drew struggled with his discomfort. He'd never expected to find himself consulting a psychiatrist about anything. Even at the most difficult times of his life—his parents' deaths, and of course Laura's flight—he'd known he could handle his emotions. He'd been brought up to function productively even when he was hurting, and to trust that the pain would eventually pass. He'd never felt the need to hire someone else to make it go away.

But now he saw that what he had mistaken, somewhat smugly, for robust mental health was really just extremely good luck. The truth was, he hadn't ever needed help because he hadn't reached that quicksand pit in his life yet—the place where confusion and frustration and fear all pulled at you, rendering you almost incapable of making tough decisions. Now he realized that a similar pit probably lurked somewhere in everyone's life. Laura, for instance, had come to hers tragically early.

"So what exactly is it you want to know?" Spencer rested his chin on the heel of his hand, and it distorted his voice slightly. "Whether you should tell her what you did that night?"

"Right." Drew was grateful that Spencer had grasped the basic dilemma so quickly. "If she knew, would it help or hurt?"

Spencer massaged his cheek absently, shoving around the loose skin that always made him look a little like a mournful basset hound. He didn't answer for a long time, then finally he spoke.

"I don't know," he said.

"Oh, great." Drew shoved irritably back against the chair and jammed his hands in his pockets. "And how much does that pearl of wisdom cost me, Sigmund?"

Spencer smiled, the corner of his mouth folding up against his hand, and scratched his eyebrow with his index finger.

"A hundred and fifty," he said. "Except you're not paying, remember? This is my lunch hour. But even if you were paying, I'd say the same thing. I don't know. Any chance you could get Laura to come talk to me? I'd feel more comfortable if I could gauge her emotional condition firsthand."

"I could try." Drew held his palms up. "But I doubt it. She's got this idea that her father molested her, and she thinks all she has to do is remember the details and, presto chango, she'll be fine. Only problem is, her father didn't."

Spencer raised his brows. "You sure about that?"

"Damn it, Spencer, I told you already. Laura was—"

"Yeah, I know. She was a virgin." Spencer didn't look impressed. "So what? Did you ever look up 'molestation' in the dictionary? It's got more than one definition."

Drew had to concentrate to keep all the ugly pictures from turning his mind into a museum of horrors. "Well, of course I know that," he said, his voice sharp-edged. "But I just don't believe it. I knew her father. He was a good guy. And Laura—God damn it, Spencer, it's none of your business, but she made love like... like no woman I've ever known. It was healthy and open and—"

He stopped. He hated, God how he hated talking about this to anyone. It felt like the worst kind of locker-room betrayal. "It was goddamn miraculous. Doesn't that prove anything?"

Spencer leaned back, sighing. "Yeah." But he still didn't look impressed. "It proves there's nothing physically wrong with her. That's important, of course. And it proves that, below the conscious block, she's still got a lot of healthy sexuality left. That's great. In fact, it's critical to a full recovery. But the conscious block is still there, Drew. You can't wish it away. And it's obviously a significant block, if it's strong enough to repress her memory of an entire goddamn miraculous night."

Drew scowled at his friend. This wasn't what he wanted to hear. "Okay, but the bottom line is still the same—what do I do now? Do I tell her or not?"

Spencer tapped his pen against the arm of his chair a few times, slowly, while he appeared to be considering Drew's question. Drew had to take a deep breath to force himself to wait patiently. The air smelled of corned beef.

"I've got two questions to ask," Spencer said finally, "before I can answer yours. Number one—who benefits if you do tell her? And number two—who are you protecting if you don't?"

Drew opened his mouth, ready to toss his easy answer at the psychiatrist. Laura, he wanted to say. Laura first. Laura always. But then he met Spencer's mournful, hound-dog gaze, which seemed to see through to his confused and selfish soul, and suddenly he couldn't say it. Oh, sure, he'd been telling himself he was protecting Laura, and it was even true—as far as it went. But at the same time he had to admit he hated the thought of telling her. He suspected she'd never forgive him.

"I don't know," he admitted slowly, spreading his hands out and staring at them. "It's complicated."

"I thought it might be." Spencer twirled his pen twice like a six-gun, then clenched it in his fist and sighed heavily. "Okay, old buddy. You're not going to like this, but here's my best advice. It's rarely a good idea to lie—even by omission—to protect yourself. The truth is hard sometimes, but it's always the truth, so by definition it's preferable to a lie."

Spencer paused but Drew didn't say anything and after a moment's silence the psychiatrist continued.

"Best of all, though, would be to get her to come talk to me first. It sounds as if she's leaning pretty hard on you during all this, so it's going to shake her up to discover that you're not entirely... trustworthy."

Drew's hand moved sharply, and he bit back a tight, low curse.

"I know," Spencer said, his eyes sympathetic. "But it's true. I'm speaking as a friend here, Drew, not a shrink. It really would be better if she had someone else to turn to. It doesn't have to be me, any professional would do. Just see if you can get her to someone."

He tossed his pen on his desk with a definitive clatter. "And then, old buddy, you've got to tell her."

LAURA stood at the door to the conservatory for a long, long time, her hand on the knob, before she could bring herself to open it. She hated this room. Maybe Drew and Stephanie were right. Maybe nothing terrible had ever really happened to her here. But she hated it nonetheless. To her, the whole house was like a hideous monster and the conservatory was the malevolent, beating heart of it.

Which was why she knew she had to conquer it.

With her jaw clenched tightly, she twisted the handle and entered. Take it slowly, she reminded herself as she shut the door behind her, listening to her shallow, rapid breaths that seemed so loud in the silence. One step at a time.

The irrigation system must have been on quite recently. The air was steamy with moisture, and the plants were a rich, luminous green that glistened in the sunlight. As she stood looking down the serpentine path, she heard occasional soft, wet plops, and all around her leaves quivered as water droplets rained down from higher plants.

She began to walk slowly, forcing herself to look at every plant, forcing herself not to panic when the curling finger of an overgrown ivy brushed her ankle. They were just plants, she told herself, nothing more sinister than that. Just ferns and philodendrons and ivy, all mindlessly straining toward the sun, completely unaware of her presence.

Just plants. But every now and then she heard a slow, swishing sound, like the drag of something soft across the path. Or a strange, hollow sighing, like the exhale of someone beside her, unseen and unknown. The heating system, she would tell herself. Or the last spurts of a dying sprinkler. Absurd to imagine the statues breathing, their marble chests stretching horribly, in and out . . . Ridiculous to think of shuffling marble feet inching inexorably toward her . . .

Ludicrous. But at every sound her heart stopped, just for a second, while she listened, and she was afraid.

She kept moving, but her nerves seemed to tingle along the surface of her skin, and she knew her control was slipping. When she brushed against the dangling, dripping cluster of a hanging spider plant, she gasped in spite of her resolve. And when, just as she reached the first of the statues, the door creaked open behind her, she let out a low, strangled cry, her heart suddenly huge and throbbing in her throat.

"Laura?"

Her cry turned into a sigh of relief. It was Drew.

"Yes," she called, her voice echoing weirdly under the thirty-foot domed ceiling. "I'm over here."

She heard his confident footsteps traversing the same path she'd taken so tentatively just moments before, and in a matter of seconds he was standing before her, irritably shaking moisture out of his hair.

"It's a damn rain forest," he muttered, running his hand back and forth vigorously, creating an absurdly becoming tousle. He dropped his hand and frowned. "What are you doing in here all alone? I thought you hated this place."

"I do." She sat on the wrought-iron bench, which luckily had escaped the sprinkler's drenching. She angled her face away from him, suddenly self-conscious. "But I've got a new plan. You see, I've decided that I may never really know what caused my fear of this place. I guess you and Stephanie have finally convinced me I'm probably wrong about Damian. But I can at least try to control the fear. I thought I'd start by just spending some time in here."

To her surprise, he didn't seem to find her idea ridiculous. He nodded thoughtfully. "It might work."

She turned toward him eagerly. "Oh, I hope so. At first just being in here terrified me. But already I'm feeling much more relaxed." Of course the most obvious explanation for her increased comfort was Drew himself. How could she be afraid of the simple hiss of the sprinkler system, how could she imagine all those dumb, nightmarish things, when Drew was standing next to her, so solid and sane and safe?

"Good." He leaned against one of the interior columns, surveying the area. "Since this room is clearly a focal point for some of your anxieties, it's an excellent place to start."

The focal point for her anxieties. She could have kissed him for the discreet expression. "Yes. I've been remembering a lot of little things," she said conversationally, hoping he planned to sit with her for a while. She wasn't quite ready to be alone again yet. "I used to spend a lot of time here, I think, even when I wasn't posing. I can sort of remember hearing Damian and the gardener talking about the plants."

Drew nodded, smiling. It obviously pleased him that she remembered something good about Damian. "I'm sure you did. Damian loved tending the plants almost as much as he loved sculpting. He worked very closely with the gardener."

It was silly, she thought, how glad she was to have pleased him even in this tiny way. She gazed around, looking for anything that would trigger more pleasant memories so she could please him again. For a moment she could almost hear echoes of Damian's voice as he and the gardener puttered along the paths, pinching off dead heads here, pulling errant weeds there.

"They talked about the plants as if they were people," she said suddenly. "I remember thinking that was strange."

"People?" Drew tilted his head, the green, watery sunlight painting one side of his face, as if he was wearing a verdigris mask.

"Well, they talked about the plants having spines and veins and throats. Things like that, like people. It sounded so weird to me. Kind of scary. And some plants were tolerant, they said, while other ones were resistant. And I remember they talked about having to coax some plants. Coaxing them..." She stopped, swallowing, her throat suddenly painfully dry. "And forcing others."

Even as she spoke, she knew she'd taken a wrong turn somewhere in the recollection. Her shoulders ached, because she had started to tighten them unconsciously. These weren't happy memories. Far from it. She had always been vaguely unnerved by the way the gardener, an ugly man with wet, fat lips, had looked when he had talked about the delicate pink throats of the lady slippers, about the fleshy, sap-filled petals of the succulents and the thick, bulbous stalks of the floating *Eichhornia*.

The floating *Eichhornia*. She wondered from what random pocket of memory she had pulled that strange name. She shivered in spite of the damp warmth of the room. Realizing that Drew was looking at her, obviously sensing her change in mood, she jerked to her feet, seeking a distraction. She moved nervously past the statue of herself toward a half-hidden bank of shelves on which Damian had always kept trays of sculpting and gardening tools.

"I remember once Damian let me chip away at my very own piece of marble," she said, talking too fast. She rummaged through the half-empty bags of vermiculite, the seedling trays and the trowels, until a flash of red caught her eye. Her hand froze. It couldn't be Damian's toolbox, could it? He had taken all his sculpting tools with him when he left, she was sure of that. It was the detail that had made his leaving seem so final.

But, on closer inspection, she saw that it was just another toolbox of the same generic style, red with silver hardware on its three or four drawers. She opened the box and found it full of gardening tools. No sculpting tools. Not Damian's box.

She was still babbling. "He let me use whichever tools I wanted, the gouges or the chisels or the picks. It was really a lot of fun." She dug her hand through the assorted clippers, trowels and weeding forks absently. "The only problem was," she said with a pretty good attempt at a chuckle, "I made such a mess of the marble it was only about six inches tall by the time I was through. And it looked all pitted and hacked up, like an old piece of coal."

She held up a long steel trowel. "Poor Damian," she said, turning it over in her hands. "He thought that just because I could sketch a little I might be able to sculpt, too. He would have liked it so much if I had had some talent—"

Then suddenly, as if someone had switched off the sun, her world went black. One minute she was looking down at the trowel, the next she was filled with a suffocating sense of imminent danger. Her heart pounded so hard her head felt as if it might burst, and she was staring, wide-eyed and horrified, at the long, sharp, serrated blade of a knife.

Oh, God . . . No. The steel flashed in the moonlight. *"No,"* she cried, but her throat was too tight, too frightened to permit passage of any sounds. She wanted to run, but her legs wouldn't move. She wanted to faint, but her eyes wouldn't close, fixed on that horrible, thrusting knife. There was nowhere to go for help, no one to tell, nothing that could save her. . . .

With an anguished cry, she dropped the trowel into the toolbox, and as she did so the terrifying memory receded. The glinting moonlight disappeared, and the green sunlight returned, blinding her. Her knees had turned to water, and she clutched at the shelf for support as she drew deep, hoarse breaths. Oh, God. Oh, God.

Drew's voice seemed to come from nowhere. "Laura, what's wrong?" Suddenly he was beside her—how long he had been there she had no idea. He had one hand around her trembling shoulders, the other roughly cupping the side of her head, jostling her, trying to get her attention. His voice was sharp and strained. "Laura, talk to me. What is it?"

She couldn't tell him. She could hardly bear to remember what she had seen, much less talk about it. She had no idea what it meant, except that it had been a moment of electrifying, paralyzing fear, and she never, never wanted to feel that way again.

She had to get out of here. Sobbing, she wrenched away from Drew, driven blindly toward the door by her fear. She couldn't breathe in this wet, clinging air, and her heart was thudding violently in her ears, deafening her. She ran without thought, ignoring the wet slapping of long, slippery leaves against her face and shoulders. Oh, God, she had to get out.

But the door wouldn't open. Whimpering like a child caught in a bad dream, she tugged at the knob. And then she felt hard hands at her shoulders, gripping tightly, holding her.

"Laura. Don't. Don't run away."

Drew. He had somehow gotten to the door ahead of her and was standing against it, blocking it.

"Let me out," she whispered through her tears. "Let me out."

"Don't, Laura." Though she struggled, shaking her head from side to side and digging her fists into his shoulders, he dragged her in closer, up against his chest. "You don't want to run away."

"Yes, I do," she cried. Why wouldn't he let her go? "I do!"

"No, you don't." His voice was low, slow and soothing. He had begun to stroke her back, though she was still writhing in his arms. "You can get past this, Laura. Whatever it is. Just try to relax."

"I can't." She choked on a half cry, half cough, and hot, salty tears fell into her mouth. "I can't."

"Yes, you can." Ignoring her sobbing, he stroked his hands slowly down either side of her spine, then back up. Then down again. "Breathe, Laura. Breathe deeply. You're going to be fine."

"I can't," she wept, but then, as if his rising, falling hands were showing her how, her lungs dragged in a deep, slow breath. She filled her lungs, but coughed, choking on the wet air.

"It's okay. Try again." He stroked up, prompting her body, simulating the motion of her lungs. "Take it deep, Laura, let it in." Mindlessly, she obeyed, opening her mouth and accepting the oxygen that pressed against her throat.

"Relax, Laura. Let it go deeper. You can take more." She did.

"Good girl. Now hold it. Hold on to it, sweetheart." He massaged her shoulders, stroked softly down her hair as she held the air in her lungs, letting it seep through her body until it reached her dizzied head. "That's it, honey. Now let it go, just let it all go."

It was a miracle. Gradually her tears slowed and finally stopped. Then, in response to his patient, knowing hands, amazingly she felt her muscles relaxing, loosening their death grip on her heart. It was a sweet relief, and she clung to him, too grateful to put it into words, to weak to speak.

She stood like that, her arms up around his neck, her body pressed against his, for a hundred breaths. Passively, she let Drew set the pace, determine the depth, the rhythm, the volume, as if she had forgotten how to breathe of her own volition. And always his hands were stroking, smoothing, easing the pain of muscles that had knotted themselves in tangles of fear.

"See?" He spoke into her hair, his warm breath feathering against her scalp. "You don't have to keep running, honey. You can beat this thing."

Finally, when her breathing was even and coming of its own accord, he twisted her gently in his arms. With firm, tender fingers he pulled her face away from its hiding place against his damp shirt and turned her so that she looked toward the conservatory.

"Come on," he murmured. "Let's go back. Show yourself that you can do it."

No . . . She balked slightly, her legs unwilling to take her forward, but he exerted a tiny pressure at the base of her spine, and suddenly she was moving. Farther, deeper into the jungle of greenery from which she had just escaped. She could hardly believe she was going back, back to where the blackness had swamped her, drowned her.

But the blackness wasn't there anymore. When they reached the statuary in the center, Laura could tell, almost with a sixth sense, that the spot had somehow lost its malignant power over her. She looked around, blinking as if she had just awakened from a terrible dream.

It wasn't that she had forgotten her vision. She could still see the knife in her memory, its curved, vicious point, its wide, notched blade. She could even remember, now, that the knife had had a strange blue and green handle, ornate and oddly Oriental, rather like cloisonné. And she was certain, deadly certain, that she had once seen that knife pointing toward her own throat.

Her heart beat faster as she remembered how frightened she had been at that long-ago moment, when the cold point had touched her skin. But, in spite of its fearsome ugliness, somehow it was a normal memory, one *she* controlled. Though it was unquestionably disturbing, it no longer threatened to steal her sanity, to drop her into the bottomless well of the past from which there was no escape.

She looked at Drew, who was still holding her shoulder with tense fingers, as if he expected her to faint helplessly away at any moment.

"I'm okay," she said, wishing she could be more eloquent. Though he might not know it, what he had just done for her was incredibly important. He had, in some wonderful way, given her a sense of power over her life that she didn't ever remember possessing before. "I'm sorry, Drew."

His eyes clouded. "For what?"

"For getting into such a crazy panic." She took another deep breath, just to be sure she still could. "Thank you for helping me get through it."

"You did it, Laura." He slowly dropped his arm from her shoulder, as if demonstrating that she could stand on her own. "I didn't do anything except block the door. You did the rest yourself."

"Thank you for blocking the door, then." She smiled weakly. "Thank you for making me stay and face it."

"Laura." In a raw voice he spoke just the one word. And then he looked away, as if he couldn't bear for her to read his thoughts. But she could read them anyway, because the same thoughts were echoing hollowly through her mind.

Thank you for making me stay and face it.

It was, they knew, what she should have done three years ago.

AFTER THAT the day seemed to hang heavily over her, pressing on her spirits just as the gunmetal snow clouds pressed on the sky. She couldn't quite settle down, her nerves humming with a strange sense of waiting. But waiting for what?

Several boxes of old papers still needed to be sorted, but she couldn't bring herself to go up and work on them, even though Drew had retired to his office, explaining stiffly that he had to make a few decisions before the markets closed.

But, for Laura, just the thought of being cloistered in the airless, dusty chill of the attic made her feel claustrophobic. She needed to be outside, where she had room to breathe, where she could think about the implications of her memory without allowing them to overwhelm her.

She took her sketchbook with her, but she couldn't quite settle down. She walked for an hour, thinking, her boots squeaking rhythmically as she traversed the freshly fallen snow. If only she could stitch the memory of the knife to some larger backdrop—anything that would give it shape and meaning. A time, a place, a person, a motive. But she simply couldn't do it. The memory remained brilliantly clear yet eerily out of context, like a jewel knocked loose from its setting.

By the time she got to the dock, she had just about given up. Her head ached from the effort to remember, and her intuition was warning her that struggling would only make the rest of the memory even more elusive. She was too tense, trying too hard. If she could only relax, she thought, perhaps the rest of it would come to her naturally.

She sat on the edge of the dock facing the house and took out her sketchbook and charcoal. She wasn't much of an artist, but she enjoyed the feel of the charcoal smoothly stroking across the clean white pages. She liked the way such nonverbal expression cleared her thoughts and steadied her mood.

She looked at the house, seeking a subject, which shouldn't be difficult. Winterwalk had been designed by one of her mother's ancestors, and family lore had it that the man had hired five hundred workers to build it in one year so that he could give it to his bride as a wedding present. Laura shivered, and wondered anew what emotions the blushing bride must have experienced at her first glimpse of her new home. Her husband the architect had probably carried her over the threshold in a dead faint.

Laura's gaze fell on one of the gargoyles, a beast she could only describe as a demon dog. He seemed to guard the entrance with wings outstretched, poised at the moment of attack, barely restrained by a heavy chain that looped around his neck. Almost without thought, Laura began tracing the outline of his flat, ugly head, sketching in the jagged horns that rose aggressively between his ears. She sketched quickly. There was something subtly satisfying about it, as if by re-creating the monster she was somehow gaining power over him.

She almost smiled at the thought, her fingers busily sweeping across the page. She was certainly big on finding her personal power today, wasn't she?

When the horns were finished, she moved to the beast's mouth, which was open in a silent screech. She quickly drew in the pointed teeth that were bared by the grimace, and then she leaned back, double-checking. Yes, that was it.

Flipping to the next page, she scanned the roofline, choosing her next subject. Ah, the terrible monkey. This gargoyle sat hunched over, hugging his knees to his chest, training his fiercely concentrated gaze on the world below him. Laura sketched his jutting brows, low over piercingly human eyes that stared salaciously at her. She was pleased with her efforts. Like the real gargoyle, her charcoal gargoyle seemed to be hugging himself in unholy anticipation of some sick pleasure to come.

And then she drew a beast man whose mouth was opened greedily. This was Laura's most dreaded gargoyle, a monster who was gnawing on a hapless, headless creature it held in its paws. She squinted, trying to distinguish details, using her memory to fill in what she couldn't see. The body in the monster's paws was rather like a bird, wasn't it? She rounded the smooth breast, sketched the rough impression of a wing, trying to capture the essence of terror and defeat that Winterwalk's artisans had conveyed so well.

Finally finished, she leaned back with a small puff of satisfaction to assess her efforts. Yes, it definitely had been therapeutic. Even with these ugly faces glaring at her, she felt much better now, much cleaner and stronger.

After a few minutes she heard the sound of footsteps crunching over the snow. Looking up, she saw Drew hiking across the white expanse from the house to the dock. He was carrying her blue coat, and suddenly, looking at the thick wool, she realized she was very, very cold. How like him to sense what she needed even before she did. She smiled and waved and then sat to wait, her back propped against the ornate railing of the dock.

"Finished for the day?" Smiling her thanks, she accepted the coat he handed her and moved her sketchbook out of the way so he could sit down beside her. She hoped he could stay, hoped he didn't have to go back up to the office for more wheeling and dealing with Ginger. But suddenly she realized she hadn't seen Ginger at Winterwalk in a couple of days. She frowned lightly. "Isn't Ginger working today?"

"Ginger's taking a couple of weeks off," Drew said, his tone perfectly calm, giving Laura no hint of any deeper meaning.

She couldn't help probing, though she knew that exhibiting so much curiosity completely destroyed any hope of pretending indifference on the subject. "Vacation?" she asked.

"Yeah, vacation," Drew echoed. "And then relocation. Ginger's decided to work in our Los Angeles office for a while."

She slanted a sideways glance at him, searching for signs of emotion on his face. His vagueness was frustrating. How long was a while? Could it be a euphemism for forever? Had Ginger been fired? Or had she been fool enough to reject Drew? Or had she just left the field for a couple of weeks, preferring not to share the house with Drew's ex-fiancée?

But she couldn't think how to ask without seeming to pry, so she lowered her gaze and fiddled nervously with her sketchbook. The movement caught Drew's attention, and he reached out to flip the pages over, looking carefully at every sketch.

His eyes widened. He glanced from Laura to the gargoyles, then back again. "I'm impressed," he said. "I thought you said you had no artistic talent."

Inexplicably embarrassed, she tore the three sheets from the notebook and began to wad them up in her hands. "I'm terrible," she said. "I don't know why I even—"

But he whisked the pages away from her before she could destroy them. Smoothing them out, he studied each gargoyle in turn, his face expressionless. Self-conscious, she busied herself slipping her arms into the sleeves of her coat and tugging the front tightly around her. The coat was deliciously warm from being carried against his body, and she slid her fingers into the cozy pockets.

"I told you I was terrible," she said finally, when he didn't speak. He seemed completely absorbed in the sketches, which she knew was unwarranted. But it did give her a chance to study him. He was sinfully attractive, she thought, in that jacket. It was suede, a mossy green that matched his eyes, and it had a fleecy collar and lining that were just about the same chestnut brown as his hair.

Suddenly he slanted her a mischievous glance from under his thick brown lashes.

"They're very good," he said slowly, "but I'm not sure you're really quite finished. I think some of the details need fixing."

"I'm not?" She couldn't believe she'd missed anything. She knew these monsters too well.

"No, I don't think so."

He looked down at the snarling horned dog in much the same way he might have looked at one of his misbehaving nephews, shaking his head and tucking one corner of his mouth in reproachfully.

"Listen, Bucko," he said to the dog. "I honestly think you need to relax, kid. All this aggression can't be good for your blood pressure."

And then he pried the charcoal out of her fist and, squatting down, smoothed the page across the hard, rounded muscles of his thigh. After a few minutes, he held up the sketch.

"There," he said, waving his hand toward the altered drawing. For a minute Laura was dumbstruck at the metamorphosis, and then slowly she began to laugh. Drew had added just a couple of small details, but they turned the demon dog into a cartoon mutt. He now wore a baseball cap perched sideways on his head, giving him the half-baked look of a goofy teenager. And Drew had bent one horn and one wing, so that they looked slightly cockeyed, as if the dog were tipsy.

"That's better, don't you think? It's good for you," he said pleasantly, addressing the dog. "You'll live longer."

Laura shook her head, still smiling. Drew had always had such an irreverent attitude toward these loathsome creatures. To her surprise, for the first time she found it contagious. "What about him?" She indicated the malevolent monkey.

Drew grimaced. "I'm not sure we want him to live longer."

"Oh, surely he can be redeemed, too."

Drew studied the monkey. "Maybe," he said thoughtfully, and then he crouched down and began to fiddle with the sketch. He didn't take long, so Laura feared he couldn't have accomplished much of a transformation, but when he showed her, she laughed out loud.

He had made only two small changes, but they were enough to completely disarm the nasty creature. He had transformed the intense pupils in the monkey's eyes by adding two dots in the inside corners, making the animal look hopelessly pie-eyed. And he had redrawn a few lines, tilting the whole gargoyle an inch or two onto its side, so that the poor beast seemed to be hugging its knees in a desperate, drunken attempt to maintain its balance.

"My turn," Laura said, eager now to play the game. She reclaimed the third sketch, the monster that was munching greedily on its victim. She studied it for a minute, then started in. Erasing the pitiful bird, she sketched her best approximation of a beer can. Then she added a slack and lolling tongue protruding from the monster's mouth.

Pleased with her efforts, she stood back with a flourish. "Voilà!" she said, backing toward Drew so that he could see all three sketches.

To her delight, he laughed with an obviously sincere appreciation. He hooked his arm companionably around her shoulder, pulling her farther back so they could view their handiwork all at once. It was truly ridiculous—three reeling, cross-eyed, drunken monsters trying to look intimidating and failing miserably.

"What do you say we name it?" Drew nudged her with his hand. "How about 'Last Call At the Nightmare Bar and Grill'?"

"Perfect." She turned to him, smiling, agreeing. She felt happy out here in the bright blue sunlight, with his arm around her, with the gargoyles tamed and her fear of them conquered, at least for today. She felt so good, so unbelievably strong, and somehow she knew she owed it all to Drew.

And then he kissed her. It wasn't a demanding kiss, or a pitying kiss, or even a despairing kiss, all of which she would have hated. It was merely a quick, warm touch of his lips, a sharing of joy, of freedom, of hope. It was, perhaps, the most wonderful kiss she had ever been given.

And then she knew what somehow, somewhere deep inside, she must have known all along. She was as much in love with Drew Townsend as she'd been on the day she'd promised to become his wife.

8

HE REALLY THOUGHT she would sleep peacefully that night. He didn't know what had frightened her this afternoon, but he knew that, whatever it was, staying in the conservatory and staring it down must have been an empowering experience. And then, out by the dock, when he had acted so silly about the gargoyles, her face had looked so young and carefree, kissed pink by the cold wind and relaxed by her laughter. She hadn't even seemed to mind when he, too, had kissed her. Perhaps, he thought, she wouldn't need to visit the conservatory tonight—even in her dreams.

Because he was so optimistically sure of all that, he let his guard down and slept deeply. And therefore he was fuzzily disoriented when he heard her soft footsteps coming across his room. He raised up on one elbow, squinting at the clock on his nightstand. Three a.m. His heart constricted. *Oh, Laura . . . not again.*

But he dragged himself out of bed, scrubbing at his face with the palm of his hand, and followed her, just as he had done the other night, across the hall and down the stairs. It was uncanny how similar her motions were, how perfectly she retraced her steps, as if she was not a real woman but merely an image projected on a screen, repeating the same scene over and over again—a mechanical glitch, doomed to eternal repetition.

He felt a sudden surge of anger. What in God's name did she think they could ever gain from this? It was insane, like some refined, sadistic torture, and it would just go on forever. Night after night she would descend into her own private hell, and night after night, helpless, he would have to watch her do it.

Damn it—*why?* He gripped the stair rail so hard his fingers throbbed. He would do anything to help her, *anything*. But how the devil was this sick charade ever going to help anybody? He stopped at the foot of the stairs, wondering whether he ought to follow her. God, how he dreaded the moment when she would begin to unbutton her nightgown. He dreaded her tears, her intense isolation, the white moonlight glistening wetly on her breast. He didn't want to see her like that again, naked and vulnerable and achingly sensual. He didn't want to feel that shameful stirring of desire, the slow burning heat that would spread through his limbs against his will. He'd taken advantage of her once. He didn't want to let it happen again, even if it was only in his thoughts.

But finally he released the rail and propelled himself forward. Ultimately, it was all about courage, wasn't it? If she had the courage to let him see her this way, then surely he had the courage to watch.

When they entered the conservatory, he held himself in rigid control, clamping down hard on any emotions that might weaken his resolve. He tried to become like a statue himself, with marble for a body, marble that was cold and unresponsive, feeling nothing, wanting nothing.

But then her fingers moved to the first button, and the muscles in his thighs began to burn. Marble, he thought. Cold. She tugged away the nightgown, exposing the curve of her throat. Something shifted low in the pit of his stomach, coiled in on itself, tighter and tighter. And then another button, down to the shadow between her breasts. He made fists with his hands. *Feel nothing...nothing. Please. Let me feel nothing.*

Suddenly, as though the projector that had been playing this familiar scene was knocked abruptly haywire, her fingers stopped. Her gown was only halfway open, but she shook her head violently, as if refusing to go any further. Though her cheeks were wet with tears, she made a low sound that, to Drew's astonished ears, sounded more angry than sad.

And then, with a visible effort, she turned, facing the storage shelves. She went unerringly for the red toolbox she had opened earlier today, and began blindly, roughly, hunting through it. Tools fell with metallic pings all over the floor around her, but she didn't seem aware of the disarray she was creating. She kept searching, searching, her fingers sorting, rejecting, digging deeper....

Finally the box was empty, the floor around her littered with the strange assortment of instruments. Drew's anxiety deepened as he saw that her face was contorted with sobbing. This was a new level of pain, and it held so much anger he was suddenly frightened. What was she seeing with those blind eyes? At whom was all this weeping fury directed?

Then, shockingly, she swiveled and began, with flailing, childlike swings, to attack the sculpture of herself. Her arms flew wildly, rarely connecting with the marble. Occasionally, though, she hit her mark, and Drew heard the scraping sound of the pedestal moving across the marble floor.

She was going to destroy it, was bent on destroying it. Why? His mind struggled, trying to make sense of it. Then the marble head rocked on its pedestal, threatening to fall, and Drew once again acted on impulse, lunging forward to stop her before she hurt herself. He couldn't let her do this. He knew he wasn't supposed to interfere, but he damn sure wasn't going to let her hurt herself.

Murmuring her name as soothingly as he could, he tried to subdue her. She didn't seem to hear him. She fought against the restraint instinctively, and the pointed edge of the pedestal dug into his forearm. A sharp pain daggered through him before he could grab hold of her fist, and blood oozed from the inch-long gouge. But he had finally captured both arms, and he held them tightly against her body.

"Laura." At the sound of his voice, the fight suddenly drained out of her, and her body went limp in his arms. She was breathing hard, and he could feel from the irregular heaving of her chest that she was still crying. "It's all right. Shh, now. It's all right."

Slowly he turned her so that her damp face rested against his chest, stroking her head just as he had done this afternoon. It seemed she was always crying in his arms these days, didn't it? But at least she was in his arms. Somehow that was worth everything.

He realized he half expected her to sink back into sleep, just as she had done the last time. But slowly, surprisingly, as her crying stopped, her body seemed to solidify in his arms. Suddenly he realized that he wasn't supporting her anymore—she was standing on her own. Her face was burrowing softly into his naked chest, and her hands had reached around him, clutching the long muscles of his back.

"Laura?" Her hands stilled. "Laura, look at me."

She lifted her head, raising her gaze to him shyly. Her lips were parted, gleaming moistly in the moonlight, and her eyes were soft and doubtful. Fear and need were burning in those beautiful eyes like twin candles. His heart pumped hot relief through his system. Fear and need—oh, yes, that was the real Laura. He softly thumbed her lids closed, and then he leaned down and kissed each eyelid in turn, blessing both the fear and the desire.

Opening her eyes slowly, she smiled shakily at him. But then, lowering her gaze, she seemed for the first time to notice the blood on his arm.

"You're hurt," she said sadly, holding the cut up to the moonlight, tracing its dimensions. "Oh, Drew, did I do that?"

He nudged her exploring, gentling fingers away. It was nothing. He couldn't even feel it anymore. "I'm fine," he said, brushing her hair from her face. "How about you?"

She nodded. "I think I'm all right," she said. She seemed to be orienting herself. She looked at the mess around them, though she made no move to leave the circle of his arms. "What happened?"

He held her tighter for a minute before he answered. He didn't want the truth to frighten her. "You searched through the toolbox," he said, choosing the least troubling words he could find. "You seemed to be looking for something. And then you began to hit out at the sculpture."

She looked over her shoulder at the sad face of the little girl. She shook her head, as if apologizing for the violence. But then she took a deep breath and turned to face him.

"I think I must have been looking for the knife," she said slowly.

He stared at her. "What knife?"

"This afternoon, when we were here before, I had a memory, just a flash of a memory, and I saw a knife." She brought two fingers of her left hand up to her neck. "Someone was pointing it at me, lightly touching my throat with it."

"Your throat—" The room tilted, and he had to work to keep his balance. His fear felt almost like anger. "Why the hell didn't you tell me?"

She shook her head. "I didn't want to talk about it until I could sort it out, until I could remember more of the details. But I think that must have been what I was looking for in Damian's toolbox, don't you?"

"Probably." Actually, he could hardly think at all. Someone had put a knife to her throat.... The image was so unendurable that adrenaline rushed through his veins, preparing him to punish, destroy whatever hand had held that knife. "But who was it, Laura? Who was holding the knife?"

She looked away, and he knew what she was thinking. "Was it Damian?" he asked. "Is that what you think happened? Is this the memory you've been looking for?"

"I don't know," she said, her voice suddenly desperate. "It seems crazy, doesn't it? I've tried and tried, but I can't remember any details. Except that it had a strange handle—" She broke off, as if horror had stolen her voice.

He felt the fear ripple through her from her slender shoulders to her thighs. "It will come," he said with more assurance than he felt. He probably would have said anything, mouthed any lie at all, if he thought it would ease her fear. "Give it time. And at least now you've got something, a place to begin. Something to work with."

She nodded, accepting his crumb of comfort like a hungry child, and as a little of her tension dissipated, she rested her cheek against his chest. His heart throbbed hard against the soft pressure, and he dropped his chin, rubbing it against the dark silk of her hair.

Murmuring, she responded with an answering nuzzle. He could feel her breath against his nipple, which he knew was tightening under the warm, delicate exhales. He took a deep breath, in which the scent of hothouse flowers and Laura's peach perfume were hopelessly mixed.

They stood that way for several seconds, or minutes... He no longer understood the normal passage of time. Oh, what were they doing? Were they mad? He was supposed to be comforting her, enfolding her in an undemanding haven, letting her rest there as he knew she needed to rest. He wasn't supposed to be running his lips over her hair, teasing them into tingling awareness with the slow drag of silk. He wasn't supposed to be massaging her back with these long, rhythmic strokes. She wasn't supposed to be pressing herself tightly against him, so tightly that he could feel the soft warmth of her breast where her nightgown was still unbuttoned.

Oh, madness—sweet, hot, flowering madness. She wasn't supposed to be making these small, needy noises. He wasn't supposed to let his hands slip down so far, down to where the slim taper of her waist flared out again into wonderfully female curves. He mustn't. It was insane. It was like walking willingly into the dungeon and lying down on the rack. He couldn't stand to go through this again. He couldn't.

But suddenly he was cupping her buttocks in both hands, tilting her against him. And she was not pulling away. Her breath was coming hard and fast against his chest. Her hands were hot on his bare back, her fingers opening and closing over the corded muscles beside his shoulder blades.

"You're right, Drew," she whispered into the hollow of his shoulder. "It is something to work with. Maybe—" Her voice caught. "Maybe it's enough for me to— For us to—" She paused, then continued. "I mean, if you still wanted to—"

Drew groaned softly. "If?" He closed his eyes against the wave of desire that swept through him. "If, Laura?"

She shivered. He could feel the tiny bumps rising under his hands, skimming across her skin. Her hips shifted, her muscles tightening subtly where he touched her. Maybe, she had said. He felt as if he was sledding down a wild, steep hill, his heart racing with the sheer, exhilarating thrill of it. But he had no idea what lay at the bottom of the hill. *Maybe.*

Oh, God, was maybe enough? Could he risk his sanity on maybe? He pressed her hips and rotated them slightly, forcing her to understand the power of his need. He heard her small gasp of shock, and his heart tightened. "You're still not sure, are you?"

She didn't answer. Instead she let her hands fall to where the waistband of his sweatpants hugged his hips. It was an act more brazen than any she'd ever—consciously—performed before. And yet there was a desperation about it, too, a sense that she pushed herself to do it.

"Are you?" His voice was almost harsh. Why was he forcing the issue so? Why didn't he just accept the sweetness she was trying to offer him?

He shuddered as she ran her finger along the inside of his waistband. Because he couldn't stand it if she was wrong, that was why. Because, though it would nearly kill him, he honestly would rather stop now than later, when all kinds of primitive instincts would be thrusting him forward. He had been civilized with Laura for so long. He simply didn't know how much more civilization he had in him.

"Laura, tell me the truth. I need to know. You're still not sure that you can do this, are you? You don't know that you're not going to start crying again, crying and pushing me away."

Finally she lifted her head and met his gaze. Her eyes were blurred, full of confusion and pain. "No, I'm not sure."

"Then we have to stop right now." His voice was flat and hard. "I think maybe it would drive me mad, Laura. I couldn't answer for what I'd do if it turned out you were wrong."

She swallowed, dropping her gaze to his chest. "I know," she said, her hand still plucking at his waistband nervously. "But that's all right."

"You don't understand." Dear God, she was like a child playing next to a volcano. She had no idea. Blind with frustration, he shoved her pelvis up against him again, twice. Ruthlessly. "Damn it, Laura, listen to me. Really listen. I'm telling you I don't know if I can stop myself anymore."

"I know." She sounded oddly sad. "And I'm saying I don't want you to."

Stunned, he released her in a peculiar, stilted slow motion.

"Help me, Drew." She put her hands on his chest, a heartbreaking, pleading gesture. "If it turns out I'm still afraid, I need you to help me get past it."

"How?" His voice was strained. "How?"

"The same way you did this afternoon," she said slowly, staring at the whorls of dark hair that curled around her fingers. "I want you to force me to face it. Force me to get through it."

Force her— His arms tightened as her meaning began to sink in. "You want me to—"

"I just want you to get me through it."

He took a deep breath. "If you start to cry?"

She shook her head. "Ignore me. It isn't really me, anyway, Drew. It's just some irrational, programmed reaction to something I can't even remember."

His lips would barely move. "And if you try to stop me, to push me away?"

She raised her face, and the torment in her eyes almost broke his heart. "You're much stronger than I am, Drew. Please. Help me to get free."

IT WOULD NEVER come to that.

As Drew carefully shut the door to the Louis XVI bedroom, he made that promise to himself again, just as he had been doing all the way from the conservatory. Force? His gut clenched. It would never come to that.

Why should it have to? He wasn't a selfish, randy twenty-year old anymore, clumsily pushing a reluctant girlfriend beyond her comfort zone. Far from it. For the first time in a long time he felt no ambivalence about his hedonism these past few years. All his relationships had been monogamous while they lasted and unfailingly health-conscious. They posed no threat to Laura now. And while they had been an emotional wasteland, they had also been a constant and exotic sexual education.

At least, he thought, he was ready for this ultimate test. He knew how to please a woman, and God willing, he could use that knowledge to help them now. Force her past her fear? Oh, no... If it took every ounce of energy he had, if it took until dawn broke on the sharp tip of Winterwalk's tower, he would lift her past it. He would make her fly over the hurdle of her fear.

Her face was pale in the moonlight that streamed through the arched windows. "I like this room," she said, and the tremor in her voice was so well concealed that he might have missed it if he hadn't been listening for it. She looked bravely lost, standing at the edge of the carpet, waiting. "I don't think anyone ever used it while we lived here."

"That's why I chose it." He crossed to her and put his fingers under her chin. "No memories. No ghosts."

She tried to smile. "No gargoyles."

"Right. Just us."

He hoped that would be true. It was, for Winterwalk, a peaceful room. But for the first time he bitterly regretted giving Springfields to Stephanie. After Laura had left him, he hadn't been able to bear living there, in the house to which he had once expected to bring his bride. At this moment he longed for his old bedroom, designed on graceful, classic lines, full of simple, masculine furniture and the subtle echoes of a happy life. This room, though the least Gothic bedroom at Winterwalk, was still slightly cloying, with its ornately carved woodwork, its heavy-figured damask walls, its gold-leafed ceiling friezes.

Its only real beauty was the French alcove bed, which nestled against one wall, sheltered from the prying eyes of the ceiling's cherubs by a canopy. He had hoped it would create the illusion of a safe and separate world.

But Laura was staring at the bed now, and her eyes were wide, her cheeks as ashen as if she was looking at some medieval torture device. He felt obscurely angry. What did she think was going to happen to her there? Did she really imagine that he would rip those silken ropes from the canopy's swagged trappings and use them to tie her wrists to the bedposts?

Never, he said again, silently, savagely. He would never let it come to that.

He shoved the heavy bedclothes aside, exposing the pure white sheets below. And then he sat on the edge of the bed. "Come here," he said softly.

She came slowly, traversing the flowered carpet as if it were a continent that lay between them, each lush rose a mountain or a desert or a gulf that she must fight her way across. His heart pounded against his throat. The moonlight reached through her nightgown, outlining the shifting curves of her body as she walked.

Finally, her breathing as labored as if she had indeed traveled many dangerous miles, she was in the shadow of the canopy, close enough for him to touch her.

Somehow he forced himself to wait. It was enough, for now, that she had come to him on her own.

When her breathing—and his—had returned almost to normal, he held out his hand. "Closer," he said. Stiffly she gave him her hand, and he tugged her toward him, spreading his legs so that she fit snugly between them. Fighting the natural urges that burned through his thighs, he didn't tighten them around her. He wanted her to feel protected, not imprisoned.

Nor did he try to remove her nightgown. It was far, far too soon for that. Instead he leaned in, pressing his lips against the soft heat of her collarbone. As his mouth met her skin through the thin veil of cotton, her muscles clenched, and she drew air in hard, but she didn't pull away.

He kissed her lingeringly, then let his lips slide across her, exploring with slow, random circles. He was careful not to be too bold. Not yet. He roamed just low enough to feel the delicate thrust of her breast against his chin, just high enough to feel the underside of her chin against his forehead.

Even this tiny intimacy made her breath accelerate again, and her fingers dug into his shoulders. Reaching out with both hands, he grasped the backs of her thighs, inching her even closer. With a low groan she bent over him, reaching down his back, and he felt the warm pressure of her breasts against his shoulder.

Lifting his head, he pulled her erect and looked into her feverish eyes. "Talk to me, Laura," he said. "Tell me what you're feeling."

She didn't seem at first to understand him. "Weak," she said after a pause, her voice small. "My legs feel weak."

"Come up here, then," he murmured. Hardly touching her, he inched her gown up to midthigh, then, when her legs were bare, nudged the hollow behind her knee. "Hold on to me," he said, bending her leg and raising it onto the bed. She lost her balance and grabbed his shoulders for support while he moved the other leg, as well.

Oh, Laura. She was in his lap, her breasts tantalizingly in front of his lips.

God, how warm she was. How easy it would be to take her now. When she straddled him like this, with only the fabric of his sweatpants between them, he could barely breathe for wanting her. He shifted, bringing her closer.

"And now?" He caressed the swell of her buttocks with slow strokes. "Tell me what you're feeling now."

Her eyes were shut, her face tight and pale. "You," she whispered. "I can feel you against me."

He pressed her in further, rocking his hips slightly, letting his heat find hers. "Does it frighten you?"

She was breathing shallowly. "Yes," she said on a sharp inhale. And then again on the exhale. "Yes."

He didn't stop. He simply matched his rhythm to the rhythm of her breathing, and though she didn't relax, she instinctively started to work with him. "But you like it?"

She nodded. She had begun breathing through her mouth.

"Tell me," he insisted. He had, somehow, to keep communication open between them. Maybe that way he could hold on to her, maybe he could refuse to let the choking darkness take her. "Tell me."

"Yes," she said between her small, gasping breaths. "Yes, I like it."

He inhaled deeply, determined to stay in control, although the rocking heat of her was driving him slowly insane. So far, her desire and her fear were hanging in a manageable balance, but it would take all his powers of restraint and concentration to keep it that way. One false move, he knew from past experience, and she would spiral away from him into a world of fear and blind resistance.

He had hoped that, because he had already made love to her once, he would be less hungry, less driven, better able to modulate his reactions to keep time with her slower pace. But, if anything, knowing how glorious it could be had only intensified his longings, giving them a color and a scent and a shape. He was like a starving man who had been given one small taste of honey. He had to have more. He would do anything to get more.

He skimmed his half-open mouth over the tips of her breasts, shivering as they pebbled under his lips. "I want to taste you," he said, knowing the movement of his lips, the warm misting of his breath, would make her nipples continue to tighten painfully. He licked out, encountering the rough cotton against his tongue. "Will you take this off for me, Laura? Will you unbutton this and let me taste you?"

Her breath caught, and she stiffened from shoulder to knee, but she brought one hand slowly to her breast, taking the topmost button between her thumb and forefinger. Nothing happened, though he could see her fingernails pressing whitely against the tiny nub of pearl. Nothing. Finally her legs tightened to the trembling point, and as a small cry escaped her lips, her hand fell roughly away.

"I can't," she said, the hint of a sob distorting her words. "I can't do it." She began to push against his shoulders with the heels of her hands. "I can't," she said, her voice rising.

"Shh." He soothed her, stroking her back just as he had done in the conservatory this afternoon. "It's all right, sweetheart. You don't have to." But his mind was reeling in a primitive frustration. Why was nakedness always the insurmountable problem? Why would she let him thrust against her in this maddening simulation of lovemaking but begin to panic when he merely suggested unbuttoning her gown? "You don't have to."

He forced himself to be calm, taking the same deep breaths he was coaxing out of her. Let it go, he told himself. Don't try to figure it out—just try to get past it. And did it matter, really, whether she was naked? His hands and lips could find her, find the exquisite honey of her, even through this flimsy layer of cotton, and it would have to be enough. There had been a black day, not so long ago, when he had been afraid he'd never be allowed to touch her again. Yes, this was more than enough.

"You don't have to," he whispered again, and without another word closed his hungry lips around her breast, pulling her into him until her gown was wet and molded to her, almost no barrier at all. He groaned as the taste of her flooded through the flat, bleached flavor of the cotton—a warm, wonderful mixture of peach and musk and female mystery.

She groaned, too, arcing her back as if in pain. Her hands still pushed at his shoulders, but she was breathing carefully... God, how valiantly she was trying, and how beautiful she looked, her face fiercely concentrating, her dark lashes dusting her cheeks, her mouth swollen, panting softly.

He moved to her other breast, suckling, in and out, in time with her deep breaths, his hips thrusting gently, an erotic counterpoint.

"Drew," she said, like a prayer, and against his will his pace quickened, his mouth taking her deeper. A liquid heat poured through him, filling his senses to overflowing. He knew they had reached the danger area. He was ready. Too ready. But if he pushed her too soon, she would panic, losing her momentum completely. Without taking his mouth from her breast, he slipped one finger between her legs, probing as gently as he could. She cried out, as if his touch was a brand, but he could feel that, in spite of her fear, she was ready, too.

And thank God for that—he couldn't wait much longer. This hot need was building inside him like floodwaters behind the wall of a dam. Holding her tightly against him, he shifted on the bed, and then he laid her back gently so that he knelt between her legs. He pulled the pillow under her head, murmuring her name, and then he touched her face. His fingers came away damp, slick with her tears.

"Are you all right?" He brushed her hair from her cheeks, where it had stuck in a swelter of perspiration. "Laura, do you want to st—"

"No! Oh, Drew, don't stop . . ."

She dug her nails into his back, arching against him. But it was as if her body and her brain were working at cross purposes, creating an irreconcilable paradox. Even as she ground her hips against his, urging him onward, tears lay in pools under her eyes. Were they tears of some complicated, intense emotion? Or of fear? He couldn't tell.

But, God help him, the deliberately sensual shifting of her body inflamed him nonetheless. She fit perfectly beneath him, and he knew she must be so close to her climax that she was floating dizzily in that dark, helpless place that comes just before the light. He was almost there himself. He could barely control his hands to slip off his sweatpants.

"Laura, Laura . . ." He wanted to bring her back, to make her talk to him again. He wanted her to tell him how she felt, to assure him that the pleasure outbalanced the fear. He wanted her to tell him it was all right, that she understood he was acting out of love, out of longing, out of a crazed, suffocating need to possess her . . .

He hiked up her gown with one hard motion, and the instant she felt the hot maleness of him against her bare skin, she gasped. He stopped, poised to enter her, desperate to enter her, but knowing he had to give her time to adjust. Slowly, with as much restraint as he could muster, he pressed.

And then it was as if his mind collapsed. He felt the tension, the incredible, monstrous rejection as her body closed in on itself, turning him away. *No. No. No.* And yet he couldn't deny it—the truth was there, palpable, like a locked door, a rejection indisputable and unendurable.

He thought he might die. Every fiber of his being screamed at him to go ahead, go ahead. She was, as she had promised, so much smaller than he, just a little doll-like body of soft, easily rent female flesh.

Oh, God, he thought wildly, was it really possible that he would even think of doing this terrible thing? He shook his head, desperately trying to clear it. It was like being caught in a riptide, swept along with no control at all. Horribly, the tide was inside him. She clearly thought it was coming, felt it in his legs, in his arms, maybe she even saw it in his face.

"Go on," she said in that stranger's strangled voice, even though her body was shrinking from him, pulling away. She wrapped her hands around the bedposts, gripping with white fingers. No silk cords held them there, and yet suddenly he felt as guilty, as sickened by the sight as if he had tied them to the wood.

"No!" He had no idea how he wrenched himself free of the tide but suddenly, in one blind move that felt like rage, he shoved her out from under him with a violence that rocked the canopy above them. With another desperate lunge he rolled away from her, and

somehow he got himself away from the bed. He stood on legs that didn't seem to belong to him, and snatching his sweatpants from the rumpled pile of bedclothes, he somehow yanked them up his body.

"No, God damn it," he said savagely, leaning his head against the bedpost, letting the brocade trappings soak the sweat from his forehead. "I won't do it, Laura. I won't."

His breath was harsh and raw in the silence. She hadn't moved an inch. She was still crying without making a sound, her nightgown bunched up around her hips, her hands still gripping the bedposts—as if she didn't yet understand that she was free. Or didn't want to be.

"I'm sorry," he said hoarsely. "I'm sorry." He tried to think, but all he knew for sure was that his body was aching, throbbing, screaming for the completion he had denied it. His lungs seemed to be made of marble.

"Laura, get up," he commanded roughly. He couldn't stand to see her there, couldn't stand the reminder of what he had almost done.

Finally a small, choked sob escaped her lips. "Oh, Drew . . . why?" She peeled her hands slowly from the posts and, dragging her nightgown down over her knees, curled up on her side, turning her face toward the pillow. "Why?" she echoed, her voice muffled.

"Because it was wrong." He turned wildly, wanting to fling the words at her, to flail her raw with the truth. *His* truth. "Because it was ugly and violent and *wrong!*"

"Not if I wanted you to do it." She made a queer little sound. "And I did want you . . ."

"Do you think that makes any difference?" He pressed the heels of his hands against his eyes. How in God's name could she not understand? "Do you really think I'm willing to become a monster just because you tell me to?"

"A monster?" With what seemed like a great effort, she sat up slowly, hugging her knees to her chest. Her eyes, swollen from crying, looked confused. "That's not how it would have been. I couldn't ever feel that way about you."

"Maybe not. But the point is that *I* would have!" The bedpost shook under the intensity of his clenched hands. Was she really so blind? What could he say to make her see? "Don't you understand? I don't want a lover who has to tie her hands to the bed to keep from shoving me away. I don't want to make love to a woman who's crying, for God's sake. A woman who has to breathe deeply to keep from fainting." He raked his hand through his hair, trying to still the rage and shame that battered against his brain, playing the scene again, showing him what he had almost done, what she had wanted him to do.

"God damn it, Laura, when I take a lover, I want her to be a willing woman. I want a woman who is as eager to be in my arms as I am to have her there."

She looked away at that, her swollen eyes lifeless. "A woman like Ginger."

He shook his head. "No. Ginger's out of my life. But it can't be like this, either. I would have hated myself, Laura, if I hadn't stopped. I would have gone on hating myself forever." His voice thickened. "And eventually I would have begun to hate you, too, for making me do it."

She stared at him for a long moment, then dropped her head into her hands wearily, as if it was all suddenly too much for her to endure. As he watched her, her long hair cloaking her face like a mourning veil, what was left of his anger slowly began to die, giving way to a much deeper sense of failure, of what a hopeless tragedy the whole thing was.

Had he failed her? He didn't know. He knew only that they had reached their final, heartbreaking dead end. It was, after all these years and all this pain, finally over. He couldn't promise her that he could live without sex, as he had when he had fancied himself her idealistic young hero. He knew better now. After tonight he knew that it would drive him mad, drive him from her, drive him to other women—or worse.

And he saw, with a fresh and tragic awareness, that she had probably been right to leave him three years ago. Her only mistake had been in coming back. He wasn't a miracle worker. He couldn't set her free.

Not this way.

"Laura, this isn't what you need, not really." He was almost glad she wasn't looking at him. He couldn't bear to see again the smoky darkness in her eyes, where the light of hope had been extinguished. "You don't need me at all. You don't need to be here. You need to talk to a professional." He took a deep breath. "I've got a friend, Spencer Wilkes. He's a psychiatrist, a good one. Think about calling him, Laura. Think about it." He hesitated, trying to think of a good way to say what must be said. "I'm sure he could recommend someone in Boston." His voice sounded odd, even to him.

She caught her breath, obviously reading between his lines.

"It's all right, Drew. I understand. I'll leave in the morning." She was still hidden behind her curtain of hair, but he could hear the resignation in her voice. So she must know it was over, too. She must know all those sad and final truths. She wasn't going to ask him to let her stay.

"Or I will. I can go back to Springfields in the morning."

She didn't look up. She just shook her head. "No. I'll go."

"I'm not helping you," he said suddenly, avoiding a direct answer. "Any fool can see that. We can't seem to do anything but hurt each other."

She stared at her fingers, which were clasped in her lap. "You didn't hurt me, Drew. You have never hurt me, never once in all these years." She took a deep breath. "And I didn't mean to hurt you, either. I hope you can believe that. As misguided as it may have been, I really thought that we might be able to find our way out of this. I really believed that there was a special kind of heaven waiting for us on the other side of the nightmares."

Finally she looked up. "We almost found it, didn't we, Drew?" She drew in a ragged breath. "We were almost there."

"No, we weren't, Laura." His voice was flat. "We were halfway to hell."

There was no answer for that, and she didn't try to give him one. He moved toward the door, his bare feet making no noise as he crossed the thick, rose-filled carpet. But when he reached the edge of the room, he turned back. He could hardly see her—the shadows of the alcove seemed to have swallowed her up, all except for the pale, poignant oval of her face.

"You say that you wouldn't ever have thought me a monster, Laura, but you're wrong. If I hadn't stopped, you would have hated me, too, sooner or later. When the nightmares came."

His eyes stung, and he bit the inside of his mouth, trying to divert the pain. He lifted his eyebrow, taking refuge in the same cynical smile he'd given her on her arrival at Winterwalk. He had to find that safe, sarcastic distance again. Why had he ever let himself forget how much it hurt to love Laura Nolan?

"And, frankly, I don't relish the thought of becoming the next gargoyle in your memory book." He opened the door. "One room full of nightmares is enough for any house."

9

When Laura finally pulled herself together and went up to the tower bedroom to pack, Drew was nowhere to be seen. The bed in the small anteroom was empty, rumpled as he must have left it when he rose to follow her. The sight shamed her—testifying silently to his uncomplaining guardianship, his disrupted sleep, his unceasing, undeserved loyalty. And how had she repaid it? With more begging, crying, clinging—the kind of scene he must have hoped he was through with forever. And then another of those gut-wrenching, frustrating sexual failures that must seem like farces to him. No wonder he was well and truly sick of it all.

But she couldn't let herself think about that, about how disgusted he had been. If she did, her heart would break, scattering all over the floor like bits of chipped marble. She'd vowed to herself that she would leave quietly, sparing him any further hysteria. She could give him that, at least.

It would be dawn soon. Through the tower window she could see the first blue pearl hint of day as it began to break open the darkness. Was he still in the house, she wondered, asleep behind one of the other twenty-three silent doors? Or had he left Winterwalk completely, to avoid any risk of encountering her again? She listened while she packed, but the house for once was hushed. Even the ghosts seemed to be gone.

She packed everything—the broken music box, the silver dress she had worn to Stephanie's party, everything. She was determined not to leave any debris behind for Drew to clean up, though her suitcase bulged so badly she feared it wouldn't latch.

There was one last thing she had to do before she called for a taxi. She hauled her suitcase to the front door and deposited it there, her purse and coat stacked on top, and then, with a deep breath, she turned toward the conservatory. Steeling herself, she walked in boldly, closing her mind to memories, shutting her heart to fear. She had to face this without falling apart. She refused to shed another tear in this house, another tear that Drew would have to dry.

Tomorrow, she thought as she passed the beckoning statue, staring with grim determination into the marble woman's strange, knowing eyes. Tomorrow she would let herself cry over everything she had lost. But not today. Not here.

It wasn't as difficult as she feared it might be. The dawn softened everything it touched, and Laura's heart beat with a fairly natural rhythm. It was a terrible room, an evil room. She didn't think anything could ever change that. But, strangely, she also knew the room couldn't really hurt her anymore.

Her lungs relaxed. Though she obviously hadn't found a miracle cure here at Winterwalk, to her great relief some residual strength seemed to flow through her veins. Drew had given that to her, from his arms into hers. And now she was going to clean up the tools she had stupidly tossed everywhere last night, and then she was going to walk out of this room forever.

Gathering silver-handled implements into her hands, she knelt beside the pond. She could see her face reflected in the glassy blackness, wan and blurred, rippling away, then appearing again, as she jostled the lilies that floated on the surface. Damian's last project in the conservatory had been to drain the pond, preparing it for a new concrete lining. In her memory she could see the muddy, lumpy shape of the empty hole in the ground when the construction workers were finished removing the old lining. It was as if it had happened yesterday.

Damian had left before the new lining was poured in. That had always seemed sad, somehow. But not surprising. If love for his wife and responsibility for his adopted daughter hadn't been enough to make him stay, surely the prospect of enjoying his new pond, however lovely, couldn't have changed his mind.

But enough memories. Laura stood, dumped her armload of tools into the box, and turning to the sculpture, slid her fingers across the sad eyes, the full childish lips, as if to say goodbye.

Suddenly the face shifted under her hand. Her stomach clenched in a spasm of irrational terror before she realized that the pedestal was unsteady and had rocked on its base.

Bending down, she saw she'd hit the statue so hard last night that the pedestal had shifted. She rocked it again, testing its balance, finding it alarmingly precarious. It was a good thing Drew had stopped her. She might have toppled the whole thing, bringing it crashing down on herself.

She tried to tug the base into place, but the marble was too heavy, and it wouldn't quite fall into the proper alignment. But she couldn't leave it like this. It wasn't safe. She scraped at the dirt, trying to deepen the hole so that she could get under the pedestal for better leverage.

And that was when her fingers met metal—cold, unyielding metal that sent a shock through her hands and all the way up to her elbows. Something was buried in the dirt.

Her heart began to thud heavily. What was it? She carefully brushed dirt from the edges of the metal, and slowly bits of color appeared under the layers of gray. Blue. Then green. Then blue again—an ever-changing mosaic of color that looked eerily familiar. Her fingers flew, keeping pace with the new, rapid beat of her heart.

Finally she lifted the long strip of metal clear of the soil. It was a knife. Oh, dear God . . . Laura opened her mouth, as if to cry out, but no noise emerged. The dirt-encrusted weapon lay in the open palm of her hand, which she held as far out in front of her as she could reach, as if the knife was something obscene she had been forced to touch against her will.

She stared at it, knowing but not believing. It was the same knife—the blue-and-green handled knife that had dominated her terrifying vision. But what was it doing here? Her mind skittered wildly, as if it was looking for somewhere to hide from the thoughts that were invading her brain.

She knew this knife. It was too unusual for her to be mistaken. She had seen it before. It was Damian's. He had used it whenever he worked with materials other than stone. She had often seen it muddy with curls of wet clay or fuzzy with whiskers of wood shavings. But she suddenly knew that the last time she had seen it, it had been shining with something wet and dark.

Her fingers closed around the sharp blade, as if she could absorb images from the metal itself. It felt strangely hot in her hand, and she shut her eyes, concentrating, willing the picture to come.

And suddenly there it was. In her mind's eye the steel caught the moonlight with startling clarity, and for one shattering instant she saw that the blade was wet with blood. Red, running blood.

Bile rose in her throat, and dropping the knife to the floor with a clatter, she rose, fighting the nausea that threatened to overtake her. Oh, what had she done? Staggering slightly, she reached a hand out to steady herself against the pedestal, forgetting in her distress how unstable it was. She put all her weight on it, and with a slow, dreadful tilt, it swayed away from her.

As if in slow motion, Laura, the sculpture and the pedestal all fell together. Greenery swam crazily, and blinding pain streaked through her body as she hit the floor. She heard the appalling smash of marble splintering against marble, and she saw her own sad face explode into a million pieces around her. And then, mercifully, everything went black.

WHEN, sometime later, Drew's face floated into focus, she thought for a moment it was another one of her visions. He wasn't even supposed to be in the house, was he? Hadn't he gone to Springfields? She couldn't quite remember. But her head seemed to be in the crook of his arm, and she could have sworn she saw him bending over her, white-lipped and grim-featured.

"Laura," the vision said. "Laura, can you hear me?" And then he slapped her cheek.

Why would he slap her? Confused, she reached up, holding her fingers protectively against the stinging, which finally seemed to bring her to at least a partial awareness of what had just happened.

She blinked, clearing her vision, and wondered how long she had been out. She decided it couldn't have been long. The light still looked weak and dawn-pale. At the side of her head something pounded fiercely, and her elbow and hip were aching in huge waves of throbbing pain. She was awake, all right. And Drew was definitely here, holding her.

"How did you know?" she asked, perplexed, looking at him, trying to sort out why he was there.

His face relaxed subtly. "Know what?" His voice had a soft, gentling quality, as if he was talking to a disoriented child. He stroked her hair from her face, carefully avoiding the knot of pain at her left temple. "How did I know what?"

"That I needed you." She wondered if she was making sense. Things still seemed a little distant to her, a little hazy. And then she saw the quizzical expression that wrinkled the corners of his eyes, and she almost laughed at herself, except that it would have hurt too much. "Oh. Dumb question, huh?"

He smiled, though a small frown still furrowed his brow. "Well, it has been a fairly regular occurrence lately."

She nodded. "I know," she said, her eyes drifting shut again. "I'm sorry. You just can't seem to get rid of me, can you? But I was going to leave as soon as I cleaned up in here, honestly I was. My suitcase is already by the door."

He made a small, almost indistinguishable sound, and then he stroked her hair again, as if he was studying the lump of pain behind her temple. His touch was so soothing she was afraid she might go to sleep.

But something was niggling at her mind, something very bad. It was like an oppression settling over her spirits. Something terrible had happened. Something had made her fall in the first place.

It came back to her suddenly, with the terrible jolt of an electric shock, and her eyes flew open painfully.

Blood. Her throat constricted, but looking up she met Drew's serious eyes. Remembering just in time her vow to avoid any more hysterical scenes, she fought for control. No crying. No pathetic whimpering and helpless clinging. She would have to tell him, of course, but she didn't have to dump the whole tragic mess in his lap, as she had been doing all week, expecting him to fix it for her.

She struggled to sit up, grateful for the bracing hand he placed at the small of her back. She felt slightly more in control when she was upright.

As soon as she was steady, he let go. "What happened, Laura?" His frowning eyes surveyed the wreckage around them. "Was this an accident?"

She flushed, realizing suddenly that he believed her capable of willfully destroying the sculpture. And, given what she had just remembered, he probably was right. She might well be capable of that—and more.

"The pedestal was off balance," she said, "and when I leaned on it everything came crashing down. I'm sorry," she added again, her voice breaking. She knew how much he loved Damian's work.

"It doesn't matter." He didn't even look at the mess. "I'm just glad you're okay. Do you think you can stand up? We ought to wash that cut."

She shook her head. "Not yet. I have something to tell you." With difficulty she met his questioning gaze, praying that she wouldn't come unraveled. "Something . . ." She swallowed. "Something terrible."

His brows contracted, deepening the line between his eyes. "What?"

"I found the knife, Drew." But where was it? She suddenly remembered dropping it, just before the crash, and she had a piercing fear that he would think she had imagined the whole thing. With a murmur of desperation, she leaned over, rummaging through the debris in spite of the way her exertions made her head thump.

Finally, with a sigh of relief, she found it and held it out to him. "This is it," she said, her voice tight. She could hardly wait for him to take it from her. "This is the knife I saw here yesterday, in that memory I told you about."

Slowly, Drew took the knife. He turned it over, peered at it, brushed away a little more of the dirt. Finally he looked up. His face was grim. "This is Damian's."

"I know," she answered, horrified to hear her voice breaking. She cleared her throat and tried again. "But it's not what you think—not what I thought. It's—" She wrapped her arms around her chest. "It's worse than that."

"No." He shook his head firmly, and his voice sounded hollow. "Nothing could be worse than that."

"This is." She quelled a shudder. "I've remembered more. When I held the knife, it was as if I could see the memory all over again." She stared at the blue and green handle, wondering what black magic the object possessed, afraid to touch it. If she was right about her suspicions, she didn't ever want the entire memory to come back to her. Tears burned behind her eyes. "It was awful...."

"What was?" He took her wrist in his free hand. "For God's sake, tell me, Laura."

She raised her chin, willing the tears not to fall. "I remember that there was blood on this knife," she said. "But it wasn't my blood. It was Damian's."

His grip tightened so hard the pain forced wetness into her eyes in spite of her determination not to cry. "Damian's?"

She nodded, the motion dislodging two tears, which ran in hot, curving paths down her cheeks. But her voice, thank God, sounded steady.

"Damian didn't abandon us, Drew. I'm sure of that. You see, I think he's dead." She closed her eyes, because the room seemed to be swaying. "I think I may have killed him."

At first a long moment of silence was his only answer. She didn't dare open her eyes. She didn't want to see the revulsion that must have settled on his features. She could almost feel him recoiling from her, from her terrible suggestion, just as she recoiled from it herself.

And so she was utterly shocked when she felt him grab her by the shoulders.

"That's the most ridiculous piece of insanity I've ever heard," he said roughly. Her eyes flew open and met his, which were glittering like hard bits of stone. "I don't want to hear any more of your suspicions, Laura. Just tell me what you know. Can you honestly tell me you remember *killing* someone?"

She looked away, frightened by his vehemence. "No, I don't remember actually doing it. I only remember seeing the knife, and knowing that Damian was dead." She winced as he tightened his grip on her shoulders. "But I feel guilt, Drew, such a suffocating sense of guilt that I can't describe it to you. I *must* have done it."

"You didn't." His voice was harsh, unyielding, his hands bruising her. "It's as simple as that. Do you hear me? You just by God *didn't!*"

Letting go of her shoulders abruptly, he grabbed her hands and, without warning, he shoved the knife between them and pressed them together so hard the handle bit into her palms. She tried to jerk away, dreading what pictures the terrible thing might send her this time, but he was too strong. He wouldn't let her go.

"You wanted me to force you to face all this, Laura. Well, now I'm going to do it." He ground her hands together even more tightly. She let out a soft cry of pain as the handle dug deeper. "You're ready to remember the real truth, Laura, you know you are. All these pieces of memories are just spilling out of you, begging to be set free. Now all you have to do is let the rest of them out, too."

"I'm afraid," she said, still trying to tug her hands away. "I'm so afraid, Drew."

"I know you are," he said, his voice softening, though his hands never relaxed by even a fraction of an inch. "But I'm not going to let you run away from this, not now. I'm not going to let you leave here believing you killed a man. God, Laura, don't you know yourself better than that? I do." The intensity of his gaze was hypnotizing. She couldn't look away.

"You have to think harder, Laura. Remember more. Remember all of it. You loved Damian. *Loved him.* Can't you remember that?"

She moaned softly. The knife seemed to tingle under her fingers, growing strangely hotter, so hot she feared she'd carry the brand of it on her palms forever.

"Remember." Drew voice was insistent, low and deep. "Go back to that night. You were only ten years old. You couldn't have killed Damian even if you'd wanted to. You weren't strong enough. Go back, Laura, and remember. You were only ten years old, and you loved your father...."

THE GRANDFATHER CLOCK was chiming eight o'clock, and Laura knew she should get ready for bed. She had school tomorrow. But her mother was out at a meeting, and Damian had just suggested that they try to sneak in a little session on the sculpture, which was almost finished. He wanted to rework the chin a little, he said.

Laura hesitated, her emotions torn. She was eager to pose—she loved the cozy talks she and Damian always had while he worked, and she loved the sweet little sculpture that looked just like her. It made her feel very special.

But she was also afraid to go. Yesterday her mother had told her never to pose for Damian unless someone else was with her. Laura was terrified of disobeying her mother. Just the thought of getting caught was enough to make her knees wobbly.

But, looking up at Damian's smiling face, she couldn't bring herself to tell him what her mother had said. It was embarrassing, somehow, because, though she wasn't quite sure what it meant, she instinctively knew it was insulting.

"Okay," she said. "That would be fun."

Damian helped her with her homework as he sculpted, quizzing her on the European countries and their capitals for her social studies test. But sometimes she could tell he wasn't listening. He'd be staring really hard at her jaw, his eyes never moving from her even while his hands flew over the sculpture. So she'd throw in something goofy, just to catch him up.

"Transylvania," she said, "Capital, Vampireville." Damian nodded absently.

Then she challenged him, and they both laughed until tears came to her eyes. It was a great game.

Then he began to tease her about Drew, which embarrassed her to death. Drew was almost thirteen and didn't know she was alive, except to express the occasional wish that she'd stop being such a pest. But she thought he was the cutest boy in the world, much cuter than anyone in her class. They were all dorks.

Damian loved to tease her about her crush. It made her mother mad when he did that. "She's too young to be thinking about boys that way," she'd say in that awful tone that warned them she was about to lose her temper. "Don't plant disgusting ideas in her head, Damian."

Her father would shake his head, looking very sad. "They're only disgusting to you, Elizabeth," he'd say, and inexplicably Laura would feel very, very sorry for him, and she'd wish her mother would be nicer.

Of course, she loved her mother, and sometimes she felt sorry for her, too. Her mother cried a lot, especially at night, when she was alone in her room. Most nights Damian didn't go to bed until it was awfully late, staying in the conservatory working long after ever one else was asleep. Laura suspected that had something to do with her mother's crying. But then, when he did go upstairs, they always fought, and her mother ended up crying anyway, so Laura finally gave up trying to understand them.

"Drew said he'd take me fishing this weekend," she told Damian proudly. Then she wrinkled her nose, remembering Drew's strict conditions. "He will, that is, if I don't bug him for the rest of the week."

Damian smiled, though he was still staring at her chin. She'd gotten used to talking to him without eye contact. "Ah, young love. So romantic."

She blushed, even though it made her feel good to hear him say it. "No, it's not," she said, shifting on the bench. "He thinks I'm just a really annoying kid. He only said he'd take me because he had his girlfriend over, and I wouldn't go away until he said yes."

Damian laughed. "Well, he's right, then. You are a really annoying kid. Chin higher, please." He twisted the sculpture, looking at the chin from another angle. "But the good news is you'll outgrow that soon enough. And you're going to be a real beauty. He'll be begging you to bug him then."

That sounded wonderful. Laura studied the head Damian was making, trying to see whether she could detect any signs of beauty to come. But it just looked like *her*, and she couldn't see further than that. She sighed, lowering her head in disappointment.

"Chin up, please!" Damian sounded impatient. Dropping his chisel, he stood and crossed to the bench. He tilted her head, adjusting by minute degrees, but seemed dissatisfied with every position. Standing back, he stared grumpily, his hand in his hair.

"It must be the collar. I just can't get the proportions." He bent over and began unbuttoning the top few buttons of her dress. He opened the fabric and folded it inside the dress, exposing her neck and collarbone. "There," he said, fiddling with it, shoving it away a little further. "That's better—"

Suddenly the air was filled with a wild flurry of strange sound and confusing movement. To Laura, it looked and sounded like the screeching flight of a weird jungle bird as it launched itself without warning from the trees. The dense plantings just behind Damian rustled and parted, and suddenly her mother was coming out of them, like one of the statues come to life, crying and flinging her arms and yelling at Damian.

"You get your hands off her," her mother was screaming, in a voice so distorted that Laura could hardly believe it *was* her mother. Laura shrank back against the bench, terrified. "I knew you were touching her, you sick bastard, I knew you were, I knew you were."

Damian's face was white, horrified, as he tried to back away from his wife. Laura thought he looked too shocked to speak. Laura was paralyzed with fear. Her mother was like an unstoppable storm, whirling through them. She was beating her hands against Damian's chest, screaming, screaming, screaming . . .

Laura never even saw the knife. She thought her mother was just hitting Damian with her fists. But suddenly something rained on the front of her dress, something that was warm and horrible as it seeped through the cloth onto her skin.

She looked down, trying to understand. It was red. It looked like blood. "Daddy," she cried, looking over to where the battle was still raging. But her father was falling, falling so slowly it was like slow motion. His eyes were wide, filled with incredulous horror, and the front of his shirt was covered in blood.

"Daddy!" She finally found the strength to move, and she lunged toward her father as if she could somehow stem the tide of fury that was pouring over him. But he was already sinking to the ground, and his eyes were staring blankly into the trees. "Daddy, no. No..."

At the sound of Laura's frightened voice, her mother whipped around, the knife still in her hand. Its bloody point grazed the skin at Laura's throat before her mother pulled it back.

"This is *your* fault," her mother said in a voice that made Laura begin to whimper. "I told you not to come here with him." She shook the knife, and Laura saw that blood was streaming down her hand all the way to her wrist. Laura's legs gave out from under her, and she sank to her knees just feet from her father's body. She started to cry.

"Didn't I tell you not to come here? Didn't I?" Her mother sounded crazy, and Laura was afraid to look up. "Didn't I?"

Laura nodded silently, tears falling down her naked throat, mingling with the blood that had splattered across her clothes. She nodded again. "Yes," she managed to say. "Yes, you told me."

Now her mother had begun to cry, too, but the noise wasn't sad. It sounded crazy. "Now what will I do? What will I do? Look what you've done, you with your selfish disobedience. Just look at what you've *done!*"

Laura didn't look up, afraid to see her mother's face, afraid to see her bloody hand. She kept her eyes on the floor, and she could see only her mother's shoes. She seemed to be pacing around wildly, her movements as driven and disoriented as her speech. Laura saw her step over her father's limp arm, as if it was no more than a log in her way, merely an annoyance. Laura moaned, low and desperate, and suddenly she threw up.

Her mother came back at the sound. "Look at you!" She grabbed Laura's sleeve and hauled her to her feet. "Look at the mess you've made of yourself." Laura couldn't speak. She could barely stand up. She was afraid she might be sick again—the odor of vomit and blood was thick in her nostrils. "Get that dress off."

Laura didn't move. "Get it *off!*" her mother screamed. "It's disgusting. Get it off."

"I can't," Laura said, crying loudly now. "Mama, there's blood all over it. I can't touch it."

"You let him touch it, though, didn't you?" Her mother's hands were hurting her as they pulled her straighter and forced her hands up to the top button. "Do it," she commanded, her voice vibrating.

And so, with shaking fingers that were so numb she could hardly feel them, Laura slowly, clumsily unbuttoned the rest of the buttons. She slipped out of her dress, trying to stand very still, trying not to cry, as if her mother was some kind of strange bomb, as if the slightest noise or movement could make her explode.

"Your dress was practically down around your waist." Her mother rubbed her face, leaving a smear of red across her cheek. Laura gagged and swallowed hard. "And you not lifting a hand to stop him!"

No, Laura thought. *No, it wasn't like that.* But she didn't dare say anything.

Her mother's voice was like a bludgeon, hammering her over and over. "It's all your fault. It's all your fault." Her mother seemed to be crying again, but it still wasn't a sad crying. It was a crazy, angry crying, and it made Laura even more afraid. She felt her mind begin to go numb, too, from the fear.

Her mother frowned fiercely at Laura. "Take off your slip, too. It's all over everything."

As if she was in a dream, Laura pulled her slip over her head, trying not to feel where the wetness made it cling to her torso. And then her underclothes, too, because they were stained, as well.

And then, shivering and ashamed of her nakedness, Laura knelt on the cold floor, crying into her fingers. She knelt there for what seemed like hours, refusing to look up while her mother kept moving around the conservatory. She heard a hundred strange and gruesome things—the metallic clank of a shovel, the sibilant sound of shifting dirt, the swish of something being dragged across the marble floor, her mother's moaning, labored breathing. Laura didn't try to make sense of any of the noises. She couldn't bear to know, any more than she could bear to see. It was all her fault....

She cried and cried, and she thought perhaps she might cry the life right out of her body. She hoped that could happen. But it must not have been possible, because later, much, much later, she felt her mother's arms waking her, urging her up to bed. Her mother smelled very strange, very bad, all dirty and sweaty and sickly sweet, and Laura didn't like the thought of her mother's hands on her skin.

"You must never tell anyone what happened tonight, Laura," her mother whispered as they climbed the stairs. "You do understand that, don't you?"

She nodded, but she didn't understand, not at all. She had already lost the memory somewhere in that endless river of tears, and she didn't really know what her mother was talking about.

But she was too tired to worry about it. She fell into a deep, dreamless sleep the minute her head hit the pillow. And when she woke up in her own little bed the next morning, she heard the maids talking about the tragedy that had struck her world in the night. Her father had run away, they said with knowing voices. He had packed up all his clothes and his sculpting tools, but he had left his family behind. There must be another woman.

They weren't surprised, the maids said, unaware that she could hear them. If ever there had been a cold, unloving woman who could drive a man away, it was that awful Mrs. Nolan.

10

Two months later, Laura sat across the desk from Spencer Wilkes, perched on the edge of her chair, her coat folded in her lap, surreptitiously checking her watch.

Spencer's normally morose face was smiling, his resemblance to a hound dog far less pronounced than usual. He looked at his watch, too. "You don't have to stay the full hour," he said, his smile deepening. "It's therapy, Laura. Not parole."

Laura laughed, realizing she must have been ridiculously obvious. Of course, Spencer knew her pretty well by now. She had been seeing him twice a week for the past two months, ever since the day the police had found Damian Nolan's body buried beneath the conservatory pond. For those two months Spencer had listened while she raged, while she mourned, while she sorted out her fears and rebuilt her dreams. This was their last scheduled session.

"It's just that, now that I've decided to do it, I'm feeling a little impatient to get started." She refolded her coat. "Of course, if things don't work out the way I'm hoping they will, I'll probably be right back here tomorrow, crying on your doorstep and begging for another appointment."

Spencer chuckled. "My door is always open for you, Laura. You know that."

She nodded. Spencer had been wonderful, the perfect therapist, listening when she needed an ear, talking when she needed a voice. She had come to him because he and Drew were old friends, which had given her a sense of comfort in his presence, but she had stayed because he was a wise and very dear man.

"But you know, Spencer, somehow I can't help feeling that things will go right." She squeezed her coat to her chest, holding in the bubbling sensation of intense anticipation. "I hope I'm not just kidding myself."

Spencer shrugged. "I've never noticed any tendency toward self-delusion on your part. Seems to me you've faced things pretty much head-on since you've been here."

She grimaced. "Well, after fifteen years of repression and denial, it was about time, don't you think?"

"I think it was the perfect time." His gaze was serious, refusing, even at the end, to jest about it. "It may have been the only time you could have faced it without permanent damage. Could you really have lived with being the witness who sent your mother to jail? Or, even if you hadn't turned her in, could you have gone on taking care of her all these years if you had consciously remembered what she did? I don't think so."

She knew Spencer was right—they'd been over this a hundred times. Obviously her mind had blotted out the whole tragedy until the last person who could be hurt by it—her mother—was gone.

Her mother. Though Laura had finally begun the long process of forgiving Elizabeth Nolan, the past two months had been rocky, full of rage. She had asked herself and Spencer the same two questions over and over again, until she had thought she'd lose her mind.

How could her mother have done such a thing? And, having done it, how could she have let Laura live all those years in ignorance, locked in her confused and haunted darkness?

After all, her mother had known, better than anyone else, exactly what Laura's sleepwalking episodes signified. Yet, night after night, she had said nothing. She had merely draped a robe across Laura's naked shoulders and led her, weeping, back to bed. She had even dissuaded Laura from seeking psychiatric help, a decision so self-centered, so self-protective that Laura could hardly believe it even now. Had Elizabeth cared nothing for her daughter's happiness—the daughter whose safety she had once been willing to kill to protect?

The most terrible cruelty of it all, though, was how wrong her mother had been. Laura's memories were intact now, and she knew without a doubt that Damian had always treated her with the normal, loving affection any father felt for a daughter. Nothing more. All the unnatural horrors her mother had suspected were just the product of Elizabeth's own fevered imagination. They would never know, Spencer pointed out, what events in Elizabeth's history had left her with her twisted attitudes toward sex. Perhaps she was as much a victim as Damian had been.

And even though Elizabeth had caused incalculable pain, Spencer helped Laura to see that her mother must have endured pain, too. Elizabeth's personality, once so strident, almost overbearing, had begun to fade on the night of Damian's death. She had, through the years, grown more and more passive and withdrawn, until gradually she had become a meek shadow of herself, dependent on her daughter for everything. And then, at the too young age of fifty-five, she had finally simply faded away.

It was then, but only then, that Laura's subconscious had begun to push the memories to the surface, expelling them the way the ocean might reject a foreign object that was ultimately too buoyant to sink. From that first episode of sleepwalking at her Boston town house to the last terrifying flashback in the conservatory two months ago, she had been struggling, little by little, to get free.

And now, perhaps, she had succeeded.

All things considered, she felt good. Lighter. And calmer, somehow, as if something deep inside her had been spinning in a state of perpetually agitated uncertainty, like the ballerina constantly twirling in her glass globe. Finally, though, it had come to a stop. That internal quiet was a peaceful, solid feeling, and Laura thought that maybe she finally understood what people meant by being centered.

"So. You look great. New dress?" Spencer was chewing on the edge of his pen. "Does he know you're coming?"

She shook her head, smoothing down the soft blue wool skirt. Spencer was right, of course. The dress was new, bought especially for today. "I only made up my mind this morning."

Spencer raised his brows. "Oh, I think your mind's been made up a little longer than that."

She smiled again. Everything Spencer said seemed wonderful today. Everything made her smile. It was like being a little drunk on hope.

"Perhaps," she admitted. "But I have been ambivalent, you know. Sometimes I feel so guilty, and I think I shouldn't do it no matter how much I want to."

"Guilty?"

She flushed. "Well, maybe selfish is a better word. Selfish for being willing to put Drew through all this again. I mean, suppose I'm wrong? Suppose I'm not totally well yet, not ready to . . ."

"Not ready to have a sexual relationship with him." Spencer had never been one to mince words, and he clearly wasn't going to start now.

Laura nodded. "Suppose it's just another disaster? Isn't it selfish to risk hurting him again?"

"Do you think so?" Spencer leaned back in his chair. "Well, let's talk about it. You're fairly sure, you said, that you are ready. Is that right?"

She nodded again. "Everything feels different now. I haven't walked in my sleep since they found my father's body, you know that. But it's more than that. For the first time in fifteen years, I wake up really rested, as if I haven't even been dreaming . . . at least, not about my father." She smiled sheepishly, plucking at her coat. "Sometimes I dream about Drew."

"Sounds normal," Spencer said, rocking his chair slightly. Laura had learned to read Spencer's little signs—chair rocking meant that he was pleased. "So, let's see. You're pretty sure you're ready to have a normal sex life. The only way to be one hundred percent positive is to give it a try, but you're afraid it's not fair to Drew to get his hopes up prematurely."

She nodded. "A real mess, isn't it?"

Spencer smiled, his smug-cat smile. "Not at all. The answer is simple, really. Just give it a try with another man first. Then, if you're okay, Drew can always be second. I'm sure he wouldn't mind. He'd probably appreciate your thoughtful concern for his feelings."

Laura made a horrified sound in her throat, leaning forward, her hands on the desk. "Good grief, Spencer, that's the most ridiculous—I could never—"

"Exactly." Spencer grinned.

She settled back, embarrassed that he'd been able to reel her in so easily. "Point taken," she said with a sigh. "Now I guess there's only one thing left to worry about. Suppose he doesn't want to see me? Stephanie calls all the time, checking on me, but I haven't actually heard from Drew in two whole months. Maybe I'll get there and find that Ginger's come back or something." She knitted her fingers together. "What then?"

Spencer gave her a deadpan gaze. "You tell me."

She thought a minute. "Well, I guess I either come back here and pay you to mend my broken heart, or..."

"Or?"

"Or I grab her by that bleached blond hair and tell her to get away from my man."

Spencer's eyes crinkled at the corners. "I vote for the brawl."

"Me, too, Dr. Wilkes." She stood and tugged on her coat, smiling. "Me, too."

SHE COULDN'T HELP slowing down as she passed Winterwalk. The For Sale sign was already up in the yard, although the realtor had told her there wasn't much interest so far. Not legitimate interest from buying customers, that is. Morbid gawkers had been tramping through by the dozens. The discovery of Damian's body had made all the papers, and everyone wanted to see the infamous conservatory.

Laura didn't get out, but she brought her car to a stop, letting it idle at the front gates. The weather hadn't improved any—March in Albany was still winter—and

Winterwalk looked a little like a frosted wedding cake. Scallops of ice hung from the roofline like icing, and the tower was covered in powdered-sugar snow. The gargoyles, all white now, too, were like parodies of the bride and groom.

Her heart felt tight, looking at this house that had known so much sorrow and realizing for the first time that it had been meant for happier things. The terrible tragedies that had happened here weren't Winterwalk's fault, were they?

And suddenly she found herself hoping that someone would buy it, someone with a lot of children, perhaps, whose laughter would banish forever the haunting echoes of a little girl's weeping. Surely someone would want it. Someone with a merry heart and a strong sense of—what had Drew called it?—whimsy.

But she wouldn't be the one. Her new life was beginning today, and it was going to have to begin in a new place. Perhaps, she thought, slipping the car into gear, perhaps she could begin it at Drew's side.

Stephanie's children were playing in the front yard when Laura pulled up to Springfields. They were building a snowman, she deduced from the lumpy ball they were shaping, although the boys seemed to be pitching more snow at each other than they ever managed to contribute to the construction.

"Hi, Laura," four voices called, a cacophony of bass and treble. "Want to help?"

"Maybe later," she said, giving Nina, who had run up to embrace her legs, a warm hug. Later. She only hoped there would be a later, that Drew would not send her away, that this desperate dream would really come true.

"Is your uncle Drew here?" She tried to sound casual, not sure what any of them had been told. But none of them, except Nina, who wanted another hug, seemed overly interested in her. The boys had gone back to their snowball fight.

"Yeah," Brett said, huffing and puffing as he dodged a snowball and then launched one of his own. "He's up in his office, I think."

Stephanie answered her knock quickly, as if she'd been standing by the door. Laura was amazed to see how huge she was, and how happy she looked in spite of the awkward bulk of her pregnancy. She didn't seem at all surprised to see Laura standing on the front porch, though Laura had not told her she was coming.

"Hi, kiddo," she said, holding her stomach with one hand, the small of her back with the other. "It's about time you showed up." She cocked her head slightly to the right. "He's upstairs. See yourself up. I don't do stairs anymore."

"You look as if you're going to deliver any minute now," Laura said, giving Stephanie a quick hug. "Are you okay?"

Stephanie growled. "I will be if I can just lose this excess baggage." She edged out of the doorway sideways, letting Laura through. "I swear to God, Laura, if this darn baby is twins I'm going to sue my obstetrician."

Laura shrugged out of her coat, laughing. "If that baby is twins, Stephie, you're going to be ecstatic."

Stephanie harrumphed, holding her hand out like a coatrack. "I bet you won't be saying that when you've got rug rats of your own crawling all over you. Speaking of which, I told you he's upstairs."

With an exasperated sigh, Laura gave up trying to make small talk. Subtlety had never been Stephanie's strong suit. She draped her coat across her friend's arm and turned toward the stairs. They suddenly seemed immense, stretching up into infinity. She hoped the knocking of her heart couldn't be heard over the squeals of children outside.

"Third floor," Stephanie called as Laura mounted the first step. "Third door on the left."

The climb seemed endless. She watched her feet on the pale green carpet taking the curving steps one after another. Her legs felt strange, oddly trembling, as if something had weakened her thigh muscles and messed up the locking mechanism for her knees. But somehow, holding on to the honey wood handrail, she made it to the third floor.

The beautiful, wide hallway stretched out before her, all pristine symmetry, white door after white door interspersed with tables laden with flowers. Behind one of those doors, she thought, Drew waited. She stood at the end of the hall, counting down. One, two, three. There—that was his door, just like all the others on the surface, but to her, entirely different.

She knocked almost diffidently, and he didn't hear her right away. She tried again, with firmer raps.

"Yes?" he called, and his voice was abstracted, as if he'd been absorbed in something. She had picked a bad time, she thought with a sudden cowardly urge to flee down the stairs. He was busy. She should have telephoned first. "Come in."

She opened the door slowly, poking only her head in. He didn't look up, concentrating on the thick pile of papers in front of him on the desk, but he crooked his finger in the direction of the door, welcoming her absently. "Sorry. I know I said I'd come help," he said. "Just give me two seconds to finish this."

His utter calm surprised her, but then she understood he obviously thought it had been one of the children knocking. From the safety of that anonymity, she watched him for a minute, absorbing the joy of seeing him again after so long. God, he was gorgeous, wasn't he?

He wore a thick, winter white turtleneck sweater, whose sleeves he had shoved up to his elbows, the house being well heated. The afternoon sun slanted across the desk, shining on his fair head and shimmering through the fine, light brown hairs on his arms. As he turned the pages, muscles shifted under the golden skin of his forearms, rippling with easy power. An answering shift deep inside her made her catch her breath.

Drew. A wave of helpless longing washed over her, and she clung to the doorknob, suddenly afraid, so horribly afraid that it might be too late. Why had she waited so long? Why hadn't she come sooner? It might have been better to come before she was sure than to wait until it was too late.

He seemed to be finishing up. "Okay," he said, stacking the papers together and adding them to the pile. "One snowman expert, at your service." He looked up, smiling.

And then he saw her. His eyes widened slowly, caught in the spotlight of the sun, which made them the clear green of a pure spring. The smile faded from his lips.

"Laura?" He sounded almost numb, and she couldn't be sure from his tone whether her appearance was just an intense surprise or an unwelcome shock. He scraped back his chair and stood, placing his fingertips carefully on the desk top. "I thought you were one of the kids."

She felt like a child, shier and more uncertain even than little Nina, who was at least able to run up and demand the hugs she desired. She forced herself to come all the way into the room, shutting the door behind her.

"I hope you don't mind my showing up unannounced," she said awkwardly. "I had gone by to look at Winterwalk, to see how the realtor's been keeping things up, and, well . . ."

She drifted to a stop. Why the devil was she making up this nonsense? If only he'd give her a sign that she was welcome. If only he would move away from the desk, come over to her, take her in his arms . . .

He nodded stiffly. "I see. You were in the neighborhood, and you thought you'd stop by?"

"Yes." She felt ridiculously tongue-tied. "I mean, no. No, I didn't come by because I was in the neighborhood. I came by to see you." He didn't say anything, so she blundered on. "It's been a long time, hasn't it? Two months . . . How have you been, Drew?"

"Fine," he said. "I've been fine. And Stephanie tells me you're doing well." His gaze dropped, then rose again, taking in her new dress, her gleaming, just trimmed hair, her carefully applied makeup. "You *look* well," he said.

"I am," she said, her heart in her throat. "I really think I am, Drew."

"I knew you would be." He smiled politely. "Spencer's a good guy, isn't he?"

She nodded, but her stomach was knotted with frustration. Was he deliberately misunderstanding her? Why couldn't they get past all these meaningless pleasantries? If he was angry with her for staying away so

long, why didn't he just say so? Even if he was determined to put an end to their relationship, she'd rather
hear that than this cordial noncommunication. Why
did he just let her stand here, frozen with uncertainty
and fear?

He must know that they had to settle it one way or
another, once and for all. When her memory had returned on that day two months ago, she had been too
shattered to think of anything except trying to find
proof, and Drew had seemed to understand her compulsion perfectly. As if the wretched scene in the guest
bedroom had never happened, as if he was still her loyal
fiancé, Drew had stood by her through the entire ordeal.

He had helped her to call the police, to answer their
questions, to set the whole investigation in motion. He
had been waiting with her in the drawing room, just
holding her hands without saying a word, when the
policeman came in to tell her they had found Damian's
body. They'd found a few scraps of her dress, too, and
with an awful irony, the set of small mother-of-pearl
buttons had survived the years completely intact.

The policeman had put one of them into her hand,
asking her if she could identify it. Anguish had rendered her mute, so it was Drew who had stepped forward, taking the tiny button out of her hand and giving
it back to the police.

"Yes, it's hers," Drew had said, his voice strained but
surprisingly definite. "I remember that dress well."

And then he had held her, pressing her face hard to
his chest, while they removed the body and loaded it
into the ambulance. He had continued to hold her while
she cried, for what seemed like years. And then he had

driven her home to Springfields, where Stephanie, the consummate mother hen, had taken over.

Laura had stayed there several days, fussed over like an invalid, soaking up the therapeutic laughing, bickering, day-to-day rhythms of a normal household. During those days the three of them—Laura, Drew and Stephanie—had talked for endless comforting hours. They had talked about Damian, about their childhood, about skating and fishing and swimming and tennis and a thousand reassuringly healthy memories that helped Laura to put her life into perspective. It hadn't been all blood and madness. Much of it had been simple and good.

But never once had Laura and Drew been alone again. And never had they spoken a single word about the future.

At the time, she hadn't noticed the omission. The future didn't even seem real. She couldn't think about anything except the past. And, of course, she had no idea how well—or even if—she would recover from this lacerating discovery. She remembered thinking, just days before, that the truth would set her free. But once she knew how ugly the truth really was, she couldn't be so sure.

Now, though, she wondered whether his silence might have meant something more ominous. Could it have meant that he had no interest in pursuing a future with Laura? He had been quietly supportive, the way he would have supported any old and dear friend, but, looking back, she couldn't honestly say he had ever hinted at anything more.

But she couldn't go away without finding out for sure. If the past two months with Spencer—and, of course, the past fifteen years of darkness—had taught her one thing, it was that she didn't want to run away from anything anymore.

"Drew, I'm trying to tell you that I came because I wanted to see you." She walked across the room and stood right in front of him so that only the desk was between them. "I've missed you very much."

His features tightened, and he shut his eyes hard. When he opened them they seemed darker, as if the sunlight couldn't quite reach all the way into them. "I've missed you, too," he said. "But I didn't call because I wanted to give you time. And space. To get better without any—" He looked down, fingering the papers he'd just finished reading. "Without any pressure from me."

She touched his hand across the wide desk, the only part of him she could reach. "Pressure? When did you ever pressure me?"

She could feel the muscles jumping as his fingers tensed under hers. "Anything I said would have sounded like pressure, Laura. You needed to concentrate on coping with your father's death and with everything you'd learned about your mother. You didn't need to be worrying about . . . about secondary problems. About us."

"Secondary? Us?" She was openly bewildered.

He looked up, and his mouth was twisted in a sardonic smile that was somehow painful to see. "That's right. Secondary. You didn't need me hanging around, waiting to hear whether you were cured, calling in daily to check on how my own interests were faring. No matter what else I said, no matter what else I meant, the underlying question would have been there, and it would have been a constant pressure. Hi, Laura. Feeling better, Laura? Any chance your fear of sex is gone yet, Laura?"

He shook his head rigidly. "I couldn't do it. I had to wait. I just had to trust that, if you ever were ready, you would come to me."

She squeezed his hand, tucking her fingers under his palm, seeking a response. "I *have* come to you," she said, her voice dropping low. "Don't you understand that?"

He stared at their hands, but he didn't return her clasp. "Because you're ready?"

"Because I *think* I'm ready." He looked up quickly, a frown between his eyes, and her heart lurched in her chest. "Because I think I'm ready, and I want you to help me find out for sure. Is that too much to ask, Drew?"

He stared at her a long moment, as if he was trying to see more than her face could show him. Slowly, as though he hardly knew what he was doing, he let his fingers wrap around hers, and they were hot and hard against her skin.

"Don't ask me to hurt you, Laura," he said, his voice as hoarse as a whisper. "I can't do it."

"No," she answered, her voice breaking. "Just love me, Drew."

For an agonized span of a dozen painful heartbeats, she was afraid he wouldn't do it. And then, with a soft groan, he came around the desk, never letting go of her hand. He took her other hand, too, and still without speaking he led her into the adjoining room, the bedroom that had been his for most of his life. He pulled her in and locked the door behind him with one deft twist of his fingers.

"Laura." He turned her gently, bringing her up against him, so close she could feel the slow, deep vibration of his heart against hers. He took her face between his hands, running his thumbs along the sensitive outer whorl of her ears.

"Love me, Drew," she said again, suddenly confused and uncertain. She wanted to show him that everything was all right this time, but she didn't know where to begin. She knew so pitifully little about these things.

His fingers were like a torture, touching only her ears but drawing a hot, slicing response from her core. "Oh, please," she breathed. "Love me."

He smiled, bending his head to hers. "I do," he said, trailing his lips along her cheek. "I always have."

He kissed the edge of her mouth. "I love your gentle courage."

She moaned, and pulling her even closer, he kissed the pulse that quivered just behind her jaw. "And I love your beautiful face. I love your sad eyes—" he touched them softly— "and your amazing smile."

He stroked his fingers deep into her hair, massaging the back of her head with a shockingly sensual rhythm. Her eyes drifted shut, and her legs seemed to disappear from under her as he dropped his voice to a whisper. "And whenever you are ready, sweetheart, I will love your body, too."

Oh, yes, she cried from her aching core, pressing against him, trying to tell him so. Yes, she was wonderfully, desperately ready. She had been waiting for years. . . . But her throat was too tight for speaking, so she answered him with a kiss. *Love me*, her urgent, parted mouth said wordlessly. She touched her tongue to the hard ridge of his upper lip, and shivered at the delicious hunger of it. *Love me now.*

She felt an answering shudder roil through him, but somehow he held himself in check. He drew away, urging her toward the waiting bed, and once there he pulled her down beside him, until they were lying side by side in a shaft of sunlight. The honey glow dappled their skin and gilded their hands, which roamed hungrily, touching and learning, wanting everything at once.

Somehow he managed to keep the pace slow, giving her time to adjust to every new stage. When her small sounds of pleasure and wonder had shifted to whimpers of frustration, he tugged off his sweater, tossed away his jeans and slipped free of everything that stood between them.

The sight of him, so strong and male and ready, nearly took her breath away, and with his gentle guidance she touched him, self-consciousness finally cast aside in the silent thrill of exotic discoveries. His powerful shoulders, roped with golden muscles. The tapering V of crisp chestnut curls that dusted his perfectly sculpted chest. The flat thrust of his narrow hipbones, the long, thick bands of muscle that bunched and tightened as he shifted his thighs under her fingers. Her touches grew bolder, more demanding. She kissed him, shaped him, loved him, as if she could fully understand the beautiful power of him only through her senses.

But soon even that wasn't enough. She moved against him, shameless in her wanting. Slowly, as if the effort cost him in some way she could only imagine, he pulled back, his fevered eyes asking the question his lips clearly didn't dare form. For answer she touched him again, and his eyes shut as his breath came faster, rougher.

He reached out blindly. The new dress had no buttons. His wonderful, deft fingers found the zipper in the back, and with one fluid stroke he pulled it down and eased it from her shoulders, down across her hips, over her shivering legs . . .

As her clothes fell away and she lay naked in the winter sunlight, without even a sheet to cover her, she felt his silence, breath suspended, waiting. Under her hands she felt the tightening of his shoulders. Below his heart she could see the rippling clench of his abdomen, and she knew the heart-stopping fear that had possessed him.

But, wondrously, miraculously, she felt no fear of her own. She felt only the deep burning of desire, the aching pulse of need. Slowly, hardly daring to believe that her body would not betray her, she rose to her knees. Drew was as still and silent as a statue, barely allowing himself to breathe. But his deep green eyes followed her every movement as she straddled him, poising herself above him.

His hands clutched at her hips, his fingers rigid, pressing into her flesh, but still he didn't speak. He didn't move. His eyes spoke of a desperate need, but the decision was hers.

There was no decision left to make. She couldn't have stopped now if he'd asked her to. Taking one last deep, shaking breath, she slowly lowered herself over him. At the moment of contact, she gasped, low and hard, and with a piercing sensation of melting warmth, of sharp, painful pleasure and of overwhelming joy, she took him into her, where she had always known he belonged. And he did, he did. Hot tears filled her eyes. He did belong inside her. Nothing in her life had ever felt so right.

He groaned, and his hips bucked once, uncontrollably, sending quivers darting out through all her limbs. She waited, allowing the small, deafening sensations to subside, and then she took him deeper still. She bent low, until the swollen, sun-gold tips of her breasts were only a whisper from his lips.

And then, although surely the welcoming heat of her eager body was more permission than words could ever convey, she told him one more time. "Love me, Drew."

With a groan of sweet release, he lifted his lips hungrily, pulling her into the hot darkness of his mouth. The waiting was over. With an instant shift, every muscle in his body readied itself. He cast away his unnatural quiescence, his desperate, rigid patience, and with a wild and wonderful abandon he took her the way she had always dreamed he would.

His hard hands held her hips, so that they were as close as two bodies could possibly be, and he drove into her with a need so powerful she thought she would weep, she thought she would scream, she thought she would fly into a million shining, glowing, pulsing bits of sunlight. Again and again he owned her, until his chest was hot and slick under her hands, until his breath was fierce and fast against her breast, until they both cried out from the sheer unbearable beauty of it and fell, still weeping, still wrapped around each other, into a black and bottomless well of perfect peace.

HE CAME BACK to reality before she did. Perhaps, he thought, tightening his arms around her, that was because he needed to experience complete, conscious awareness of every miraculous second. Perhaps, in spite of everything that had happened, he secretly feared it would disappear, feared that it could somehow, even now, be taken away from him.

But when he touched her, she was reassuringly warm. So marvelously real. Her head lay against his chest, her dark hair spread out like silk over his shoulders. There was something incredibly innocent about the way she had, in her exhaustion, slid with a sigh to the bed beside him. She had murmured a low sound of intense satisfaction, and then she had curled trustingly in the crook of his arm, her knee thrown over his thigh, her hand pressed against his chest, as if she wanted to feel his heart throbbing against her palm while she slept.

He looked down at the lovely, peaceful profile that nuzzled against him, totally unaware of being observed. Not many people, he thought, could have endured such ordeals and still possess such heartbreaking innocence and beauty.

Suddenly, foolishly, his eyes stung, and he blinked back the burning wetness angrily. He had never cried for her before. Why now, when her ordeal was finally over, did he find himself unable to bear the thought of how terrible it must have been? He stroked the velvety dampness of her back, marveling at the deceptive fragility of her delicate bones, the childish, rosy pout of her parted lips. No, this was no fragile child. This was a woman of amazing passion, indomitable spirit. How brave she was. How courageously she had struggled against the demons that had threatened to destroy her life.

And how sweetly she had come to share the fruits of her victory with him. Gratitude was like a physical ache within his chest. He knew himself to be a lucky man. He tightened his arms even more, as if he would physically block any pain that tried to reach her from this moment forward.

She stirred, and he knew he had awakened her. She sighed softly, her breath warm and tingling against his sensitized skin. She stretched her back, arching in unconscious sensuality, and he felt himself start to want her all over again.

She ran her foot along the curve of his calf. "That was nice," she murmured, and he could hear the throaty, teasing understatement in her voice. She hadn't had enough, either. He could feel it in the slight tension of her thighs.

"Yes, it was," he said in a similar tone, letting his hand feather down to the small of her back. "Very."

She snuggled closer. "Better, I think, than before."

His hand froze, his fingers going abruptly numb. "Before?"

She had begun to play with the hair on his chest, drawing small, tickling circles around his pebbling nipple. "Yes, well, that tiny cot wasn't really as comfortable as this big, lovely bed, was it?"

The cot . . .

"Laura . . ." With one swift, urgent motion, he rotated her onto her back and rose onto his elbows above her. He looked at her soft blue eyes with a gaze full of questioning incredulity. "I thought you didn't remember that night," he said. "I thought you weren't really awake."

She smiled up at him. "I wasn't."

Then what—how? He cursed, low and intense, a shock of betrayal coursing through him. "Spencer told you?"

She frowned slightly. "Did Spencer know?"

"I went to him," he said, anger making his voice tight. "Right after it happened. I didn't know what to do, whether to tell you, whether it would be worse if you realized what you had done. But, damn it, he knew I was talking to him in confidence. He knew I wouldn't have wanted him to tell you—"

She hushed him with one soft fingertip. "It wasn't Spencer," she said gently. "Spencer would never have said a word, you know that. But you see, the amazing thing about unblocking your memories is that you don't get just a select few. You don't call them up by the year you want, or the person you want, or the place or the type, like files from a computer. Apparently you get them all, the little and the big, the good and the bad." She traced the curve of his lower lip. "At least I did."

"Oh, God." He could hardly meet her eyes. "I'm sorry, Laura," he said, his heart sinking under its burden of guilt. He should have told her. He shouldn't have left her to remember on her own, to suffer that new betrayal without any warning, without any explanation.

"There is no excuse for what I did. All I can say is that I really didn't know, Laura, I swear I didn't. I should have, but I didn't. You seemed so normal. Your eyes were open, and you spoke to me, you said my name with all the longing I'd always wanted to hear."

He swallowed, his throat catching on something jagged. "I guess that's the selfish, simple truth of it, Laura. I wanted to believe it was the real you."

She smiled again, almost dreamily. "It *was* the real me. Don't you see that? It was what I could be when the terror set me free, when it was just you and me and all the love there was between us." Her eyes shone wetly, and her smile trembled. "Don't regret it, Drew. That memory got me through the past two months. Knowing love could be so beautiful, even for me, gave me the courage to keep trying."

He wasn't sure he could speak. The lump in his throat seemed to be in the way of the words. "But I didn't tell you, even when I realized what I'd done. Can you ever forgive me for that?"

She touched his cheek. "Well," she said softly, "it is a good thing I remembered. It might have been rather awkward...."

He tilted his head. "Awkward?"

"Explaining to my doctor." She lay both hands on her stomach and looked up at him. "Explaining how I could possibly be expecting a baby in the fall."

His arms almost gave way under his weight. Just in time he rolled away from her and fell back against the pillows, his heart thudding violently in his chest. He couldn't believe his ears. He couldn't believe...

But then, with a gentle murmur, she took his hand and placed it on the smooth, warm skin of her belly. "It's true," she said. "We made a child that night, Drew, that night in the tower. It's growing now, right here under my heart."

His fingers were stiff. "But a baby... Laura, it's so unfair...to you... You didn't even know what you were doing."

She chuckled softly and began to guide his hands in slow strokes across her stomach. "And still I got it right." She moved his hand lower. "It must mean I'm a natural, don't you think?"

He halted their drifting fingers before she took him too far, past the point at which he knew he could never stop.

"It means you are a miracle. My miracle." Leaning over her, he dipped his head to her shoulder, shutting his eyes and brushing his lips across the satin of her skin. His wife. His child. His family. His dream. All rescued from the ashes by one mad night of thoughtless passion, a night he had dared to rue. Joy was like a piercing light, and it brought with it a surge of desire so strong it almost blinded him.

"We'll start over," he said suddenly. "I'll build you a new home, Laura, a home for you and the baby." He tucked her body beneath his and pressed against her, showing her how she made him feel, how thrilling he found her fertile warmth, her gift of new life, new hope, new love. "I'll take you somewhere warm and golden, somewhere without snow or ghosts or winter. I'll find a place where it's always summer, where miracles always come true."

"You don't have to take me anywhere, Drew," she said, smiling as she opened for him, body, heart and soul. "We've found that place already."

Epilogue

LAURA WOKE UP slowly, gathering a gradual awareness of the peach-colored dawn filtering through the lace curtains. Instinctively, as she did every morning, she wriggled backward until she met the warm strength of Drew's body. Without waking, Drew murmured and automatically reached for her, wrapping his hand across her stomach. Nestling there, spooned tightly against him, she shut her eyes and smiled. No wonder she never walked in her sleep anymore. Why would she ever willingly leave such a blissful haven? It was a miracle she ever got up at all.

Of course the twins would have something to say about that. At almost four years old, they had something to say about almost everything. She pictured them now, asleep in their tumbled beds across the hall, their limbs splayed in innocent abandon, their chestnut hair sticking out every which way like tossed straw, their mischievous, darling faces for once peaceful and still. They would be awake soon, the peace shattered by laughter and Indian whoops, by race cars vrooming over hardwood floors, by plastic dinosaurs thundering across prehistoric mountains of Legos.

Oh, yes, they'd have plenty to say if their parents refused to get out of their cozy bed. *I'm hungry. I can't find my cars. I want to play catch. You promised you'd*

*lift me up to see the birds' nest. You said we could go
out on the lake today.*

She smiled, thinking of the din two little boys could
create. And what would they say, she wondered, snug-
gling closer to Drew, when they heard about the new
baby? Last night she and Drew had decided that it was
time to share the news. They would tell the boys today.

She put her hand over Drew's, over the barely per-
ceptible swell that was the baby, and suddenly she knew
what had awakened her so early. A tiny flutter moved
against her ribs, like a ripple skimming the surface of
the lake. Her smile deepened, and she tightened Drew's
hand against her. The baby, Drew, she wanted to say.
I felt the baby move.

But she let him sleep. It was too soon, the movements too subtle for him to share yet. In a couple of
months, Drew would marvel in them, just as he had in
the rambunctious wrigglings of his twin sons. This time
the boys would put their tiny hands on her stomach,
too. She could imagine how they would laugh when
their little, unseen sister kicked against them. She could
hardly wait. For now, though, it was her own private
miracle.

Just one of many miracles. She opened her eyes and
gazed lovingly around her beautiful room. Simple and
open, bright and sunny now as the dawn gave way to
the golden glow of a cloudless summer day. Summer-
land, they called it, this big, rambling Florida house on
Lake Mercy, with a wide porch that ran across the second story. She loved that porch. She and the boys often sat up there on hot afternoons, lazing on the swing,
telling stories and singing songs, watching the sun
dance across the glittering lake while they waited for

Drew to come back from a meeting or a day at the office.

He was never gone overnight. She knew it required elaborate professional manipulations, but he always managed to get home in time to tuck the boys in bed, in time to hold her as she fell asleep. When she tried to assure him that she'd be okay alone, that she was no longer afraid to face her dreams, he'd merely shake his head.

"It's not for you," he'd lie with a smile. "It's for me. I can't sleep without you anymore."

And she loved him all the more for the lie, for the constancy with which he guarded her even now that she needed no guarding. And besides, she didn't want him to stay away. After four and a half years of marriage, they still turned to each other every night, hungry to touch and be touched, to love and be loved.

That was the most wondrous miracle of all, she thought, spooning herself even closer, so close she could feel the warm exhale of his sleeping breath against her ear. At first Drew had been painfully careful not to push her, to wait until she asked for his touch, always watching for signs of fear, of the old panic and rejection. But those things were gone forever, and finally believing in her recovery, he had begun to reach out freely, without censoring himself, giving in completely to the moment.

And what moments they were! Sex was sometimes joyous, bubbling over into a silly, frolicking romp; sometimes soapy and hot and languorous as they stood together in the shower. Sometimes he came to her at midnight, wild and wicked, tearing her clothes and taking her on the floor, and sometimes he wakened her before dawn with a sleepy loving that seemed as soft and delicious as a dream.

Sometimes, though, the past seemed to hang in the room like sad, slow music, and his eyes were dark and desperate. On those nights his lovemaking would be silent, reverent, frightened, grateful, profound. And she would know he was remembering how close their miracle had come to dying.

She pressed herself against him, as if to reassure herself all this happiness was real.

"If you don't stop wiggling your sexy bottom like that," Drew growled suddenly against her ear, his voice throaty with sleep, "I won't answer for the consequences." Grinning into her pillow, she made a slow, deliberate circle with her hips.

His hands tightened on her belly. "Shameless hussy," he whispered, nipping at her ear and doing some rather subtle wriggling of his own. Her breath came quickly as he slid his fingers seductively across the cotton nightgown she wore, searching for the hem and pulling it up around her thighs. He tilted her hips, and she sighed happily.

"Absolutely shameless," she agreed, her body moving under his hands, her heart pounding in her ears so loudly she almost didn't hear the muffled voices in the room across the hall.

"I'm going to tell Daddy you smashed my castle!"

"I did not! Your dumb castle just fell down 'cause you made it wrong!"

"It was not a dumb castle!"

"Was too!"

"I'm telling Daddy!"

Her heart slowing reluctantly, Laura cast a mournful look over her shoulder at Drew, who dropped his head against the pillow and squeezed his eyes shut. "Quick," he said. "Lock the door."

"Too late," Laura said as the sound of scuffling boys grew louder. "I guess we'll just have to wait."

Drew groaned. "I don't think I can."

She sat up, arranging her nightgown demurely. "Of course you can." She patted his shoulder. "You waited years, remember? You have more patience than any man I know."

"That's just it," he said morosely, though his eyes twinkled at her. "I used it up. I'm out."

Laura didn't have time to answer. Twin cyclones burst into the room, whirling toward them noisily, their grievances thankfully forgotten somewhere on the way to their parents' bedroom. The boys tumbled onto the bed, kissing and laughing and demanding the loving attention they had always taken for granted. This was what she had wanted for her children, she realized, this boisterous belief that they were always welcome. Watching Drew hug his sons, Laura's heart felt suddenly full to overflowing.

"Take us somewhere," the boys clamored, tugging at the sheets, urging their lazy parents to get up.

And Drew, winking at Laura, answered dryly, "Okay, you can come with me to the patience store."

The boys looked confused and slightly disappointed. "That doesn't sound like very much fun," Nolan said, screwing up his mouth.

And Stephen nodded. "Sounds boring," he said emphatically.

"All right, then," Drew said philosophically, settling a boy on each side of him. "Somewhere else, then." He smiled at Laura, the smile that always made her melt inside. "I know. Let's go to the baby store."

Nolan's skeptical disgust didn't lessen, but Laura noticed that Stephen looked suddenly curious. "The baby store?"

Nolan snorted. "We're not babies anymore."

Drew looked his question at Laura, and she nodded, her throat tight with silly tears.

He drew a deep breath. "Boys," Drew said solemnly, "your mother has something wonderful to tell you."

HARLEQUIN®

Temptation

Secret Fantasies

Do you have a secret fantasy?

Celebrity author and recluse Emma Jordan does. She
is collaborating on a screenplay of her bestselling
erotic thriller with talented, sexy-as-sin Sam Cooper.
Once he's gone, she knows she'll never see him again.
He'll be playing the starring role in their movie…just
as he has been in her fantasies…. Experience the
seduction in #526 *Obsession* (February 1995), by a
fabulous new writer, Debra Carroll.

Everybody has a secret fantasy. And you'll find
them all in Temptation's exciting new yearlong
miniseries, **Secret Fantasies**. Beginning January 1995,
one book each month focuses on the hero or
heroine's innermost fantasy….

Where do you find hot Texas nights, smooth Texas charm and dangerously sexy cowboys?

Crystal Creek reverberates with the exciting rhythm of Texas. Each story features the rugged individuals who live and love in the Lone Star state.

"...Crystal Creek wonderfully evokes the hot days and steamy nights of a small Texas community...impossible to put down until the last page is turned." —*Romantic Times*

Praise for Bethany Campbell's *Rhinestone Cowboy*

"...this is a poignant, heart-warming story of love and redemption. One that Crystal Creek followers will wish to grab and hold on to." —*Affaire de Coeur*

"Bethany Campbell is surely one of the brightest stars of this series." —*Affaire de Coeur*

Don't miss the final book in this exciting series. Look for **LONESTAR STATE OF MIND** by BETHANY CAMPBELL

Available in February wherever Harlequin books are sold.

MOVE OVER, MELROSE PLACE!

> Apartment for rent
> One bedroom
> Bachelor Arms
> 555-1234

Come live and love in L.A. with the tenants of Bachelor Arms. Enjoy a year's worth of wonderful love stories and meet colorful neighbors you'll bump into again and again.

First, we'll introduce you to Bachelor Arms' residents Josh, Tru and Garrett—three to-die-for and determined bachelor buddies—who do everything they can to avoid walking down the aisle. These three romantic comedies, written by bestselling author Kate Hoffmann, kick off this fabulous new continuity series from Temptation:

BACHELOR HUSBAND #525 (February 1995)

THE STRONG SILENT TYPE #529 (March 1995)

A HAPPILY UNMARRIED MAN #533 (April 1995)

Soon to move into Bachelor Arms are the heroes and heroines in books by our most popular authors—JoAnn Ross, Candace Schuler and Judith Arnold. You'll read a new book every month.

Don't miss the goings-on at Bachelor Arms

HARLEQUIN®

Deceit, betrayal, murder

Join Harlequin's intrepid heroines, India Leigh
and Mary Hadfield, as they ferret out the truth
behind the mysterious goings-on in their
neighborhood. These two women are no milk-
and-water misses. In fact, they thrive on

MISCHIEF & MAYHEM

Watch for their incredible adventures in this
special two-book collection. Available in March,
wherever Harlequin books are sold.

Fifty red-blooded, white-hot, true-blue hunks
from every State in the Union!

Look for MEN MADE IN AMERICA! Written by some
of our most popular authors, these stories feature some
of the strongest, sexiest men, each from a different state
in the union!

Two titles available every month at your favorite
retail outlet.

In January, look for:

WITHIN REACH by Marilyn Pappano (New Mexico)
IN GOOD FAITH by Judith McWilliams (New York)

In February, look for:

THE SECURITY MAN by Dixie Browning
(North Carolina)
A CLASS ACT by Kathleen Eagle
(North Dakota)

You won't be able to resist MEN MADE IN AMERICA!

Bestselling Author

Elise Title

Anything less than everything is not enough.

Coming in January 1995, Sylver Cassidy and Kate Paley take
on the movers and shakers of Hollywood. Young, beautiful,
been-there, done-it-all type women, they're ready to live by their
own rules and stand by their own mistakes. With love on the
horizon, can two women bitten by the movie bug really have it
all? Find out in

HOT
PROPERTY

 MIRA The brightest star in women's fiction

METHP

HARLEQUIN®

Don't miss these Harlequin favorites by some of our most
distinguished authors!
And now, you can receive a discount by ordering two or more titles!

HT#25577	WILD LIKE THE WIND by Janice Kaiser	$2.99	☐
HT#25589	THE RETURN OF CAINE O'HALLORAN by JoAnn Ross	$2.99	☐
HP#11626	THE SEDUCTION STAKES by Lindsay Armstrong	$2.99	☐
HP#11647	GIVE A MAN A BAD NAME by Roberta Leigh	$2.99	☐
HR#03293	THE MAN WHO CAME FOR CHRISTMAS by Bethany Campbell	$2.89	☐
HR#03308	RELATIVE VALUES by Jessica Steele	$2.89	☐
SR#70589	CANDY KISSES by Muriel Jensen	$3.50	☐
SR#70598	WEDDING INVITATION by Marisa Carroll	$3.50 U.S. $3.99 CAN.	☐
HI#22230	CACHE POOR by Margaret St. George	$2.99	☐
HAR#16515	NO ROOM AT THE INN by Linda Randall Wisdom	$3.50	☐
HAR#16520	THE ADVENTURESS by M.J. Rodgers	$3.50	☐
HS#28795	PIECES OF SKY by Marianne Willman	$3.99	☐
HS#28824	A WARRIOR'S WAY by Margaret Moore	$3.99 U.S. $4.50 CAN.	☐

(limited quantities available on certain titles)

	AMOUNT	$
DEDUCT:	10% DISCOUNT FOR 2+ BOOKS	$
ADD:	POSTAGE & HANDLING	$
	($1.00 for one book, 50¢ for each additional)	
	APPLICABLE TAXES*	$_____
	TOTAL PAYABLE	$_____
	(check or money order—please do not send cash)	

To order, complete this form and send it, along with a check or money order for the
total above, payable to Harlequin Books, to: **In the U.S.:** 3010 Walden Avenue,
P.O. Box 9047, Buffalo, NY 14269-9047; **In Canada:** P.O. Box 613, Fort Erie, Ontario,
L2A 5X3.

Name:_____

Address: _____ City:_____

State/Prov.: _____ Zip/Postal Code: _____

*New York residents remit applicable sales taxes.
 Canadian residents remit applicable GST and provincial taxes.

HBACK-JM2